That Old Time Religion

Will A. Sanborn

Thank you to the fans of my work who continue to support me in my creative endeavors. Your comments and feed-back are always appreciated.

Thank you Heather as well, for sharing your artistic vision to help illuminate the world and characters of this story.

Published by WAS1 Productions
http://www.was1.net

Printed by Lulu Print-on-Demand Publishing
http://www.lulu.com

Written as part of National Novel Writing Month
http://www.nanowrimo.org

Table of Contents

Chapter 1: Who Mourns for Anubis? 3

Chapter 2: Welcome to the Jungle 7

Chapter 3: Going Down the Rabbit Hole 15

Chapter 4: Good Morning, There's Something You Should Know 25

Chapter 5: On the Road Again 31

Chapter 6: Breakfast of the Gods 39

Chapter 7: Take Some Time with a Friend, Take Some Time for Love.. 47

Chapter 8: Yet Another Revelation.. 57

Chapter 9: Time out for Fun 73

Chapter 10: Trying it on the Other Side 85

Chapter 11: St. Pauli Girl 97

Chapter 12: Norse Meets West...105

Chapter 13: A Glimmer of Hope, a Shadow of Doubt............................ 113

Chapter 14: The Moment of Truth 125

Chapter 15: Aftermath 135

Epilogue: Incognito in Plain Sight 141

Author's Notes

I have some fond memories from this story. It was written as part of the National Novel Writing Month challenge, back in November of 2003. Working on "That Old Time Religion" helped me get out of a big writing slump I was in at the time. I'd heard of NaNoWriMo before, but that year I decided to give it a chance. I hadn't written much of anything in awhile and I hadn't done a novel-length project since writing "The Journey" many years before. I tend to like shorter stories better, but it was good to get back into a longer project. I started with a glimmer of some ideas and it was a wonderful adventure seeing where it would take me.

There was some writing that was done to pad out the story to get the word-count up, but it's all good. Looking back at it now, it does all work together to tell the story, and even the side trips helped flesh out the situations and characters. There are two chapters of love scenes which could possibly have happened off camera. However, besides being fun to write and I imagine fun to read as well, they do have elements which are organic to the plot and the characters' relationships.

In re-reading and editing the novel again, I was happy to see that the story works well in three acts: the set-up of the situation, character interactions and growth, and the final action in the end. Some aspects of the relationships may have happened a little quickly, but I think I was true to how the characters felt to me and I worked at making the romantic and erotic scenes believable.

Anubis was a fun character to write. He started off as both a nod to and a slight poke at how the Egyptian god is portrayed in the furry fandom. While I'd admit it is a little silly to see how much adult attention he gets, I also find his depictions in the artwork attractive and fun. I knew I wanted to do something with him here and it was entertaining to see how he grew into a fully-realized character. He may be a little emotional, but he's also quite warm and caring. He and Thoth made a good odd couple to pair up. All of the characters evolved nicely and provided the story will lots of emotional impact.

Finally, some people might have wondered about the use of exotics in this novel. I wanted a different word than just "furries" to use in my stories, so I came up with that term. I think it's descriptive enough, and more evocative and less cumbersome than "anthropomorphic animals." When I used the term in my short story "Faded Celluloid Dreams" I'd alluded to the exotics being engineered beings, for use in the entertainment industry. Here though, I wanted to suggest that exotics were offshoots of genetics that occurred naturally. I liked the idea of a world populated by both humans and furries, so I tried to allude to that with the exotics. Of course it was necessary for this novel, given how some of the characters have to pose as mortals.

Will A. Sanborn

Chapter 1: Who Mourns for Anubis?

Every time I turn around, a year has passed me by
If only we could stop it for a while
It all goes by so fast, now becomes the past
It all goes by so fast, and we're never going back
   Thanks to Gravity, "It All Goes by so Fast"

Once I walked a moonlit desert, by shooting stars I felt my pleasure
Now my heart is insulated, I guess my soul is slightly jaded
But I will find the time one day, to expose these wires again
I think I can...
   Thanks to Gravity, "Get Used To"

The music rolled over him like a wave as he entered the club, with the loud rhythmic pounding bass surrounding him. The noise or the pulsating lights didn't hit him as hard as the smells though. He'd gotten used to that from dealing with the crowding of the cities in this new age of man, but the effects could still be overwhelming, at least briefly. There was the scent of male excitement in the air, mixed with the stink of smoke which overpowered it. The former he was not impartial to, but the latter assaulted his sensitive nostrils.

He took a deep breath, drawing the air into his lungs, to acclimate to the new environment. Once he was over the original shock, the effect wasn't too bad. He still wouldn't have chosen this venue under normal circumstances though. Even after all this time he didn't like crowds. He reminded himself why he was there and walked into the fray. He could feel the eyes upon him as he walked through the crowd, but the attention was brief. He'd managed to get a second look from the handsome gentleman guarding the doors, and that was more than usual. Unable to know his true identity, most people took him as another exotic, and as an exotic, being a humanoid avian wasn't usually considered attractive. It was the felines and canids who got most of the attention.

That was just as well though, since he wasn't there to pick up someone. He wasn't interested in that diversion just then, his goal was much more focused. As his eyes adjusted to the flashing lights, the ibis-headed figure moved slowly along, moving his head from side to side, scanning for a familiar face. The majority of the patrons were human, as was to be expected, but this was the city, so there were some exotics among the dancing, mingling bodies. They were easy to spot, and that made his job easier, as he was looking for someone who stood out, like himself.

After he'd walked along the perimeter of the dance floor, having ignored a couple of half-hearted attempts from strangers trying to flirt with him, he could tell the male he was looking for was not there. He wasn't out on the floor at least. That didn't rule out the other areas though. He noted the tables off against the walls and continued his search in that direction. A few minutes later he'd spied him, a figure who appeared to be a jackal exotic, sitting alone in a dark corner, nursing a drink. That was about typical of him, especially in the state he was apt to be in.

Making his way through the crowd, the avian reached the seated jackal. He'd approached him from the side, so his old friend hadn't seen him. It wasn't until he'd gently laid a hand on the dark canine's shoulder that the jackal had registered his presence.

The jackal turned his head to look up at him; the look of hopeful expectation quickly vanished from his face, to be replaced by surprise. "Thoth, it's you!" he exclaimed as his ears flicked with excitement. "What are you doing here?"

"Looking for you, Anubis" the ibis replied, as he took a seat next to him. The music wasn't as overwhelming back where they were, but it was still loud enough that they needed to talk with their voices raised. He saw the slight gleam in the jackal's eyes as he answered him; no doubt his old friend was relieved to be looking upon a familiar face once again. "But what are you doing here? This is a bit below your usual venues, isn't it?"

Anubis' expression paled slightly. He took a moment to answer, but finally came back with "I needed to be with someone... It's been too long."

Thoth nodded and reached out to touch his old friend's hand. "You could always come back, you don't have to go wandering like this."

"No, that only reminds me of what's been lost."

"So you'd rather drift along as a stranger, than be with your heritage?"

Anubis' ears tilted backwards. "What heritage Thoth? There's nothing left for us in Egypt but ruins. I'd rather spend my time with the living anyway. They don't need us anymore, but they are still vital."

Thoth shook his head slightly. "I wish you could learn to enjoy the afterlife like all of the people you helped to bring there. We had our time, and the torch has been passed."

"But the dynasty was supposed to last for ever, Thoth."

"No, even you know that nothing in this world is eternal. You've seen other great empires fall, just as ours did." He paused as he looked into the jackal god's eyes, studying him. "Just what are you looking for, Anubis? You can't have consorts like you were able to in the old days. I don't think anybody would be all that interested in bedding an ancient god of funerary practices, much less believe you if you told them who you were." He stopped, having seen his friend's reaction, and instantly regretted his words.

Anubis glanced down, breaking eye contact from Thoth. "I know... but it's been so lonely. I figured that people would appreciate this form at least, like they do with the exotics. I just needed to have someone touch me... I want to feel like I have a purpose again, even if just for a night."

Will A. Sanborn

Thoth squeezed his hand, and as Anubis looked back up at him, the ibis god could see the jackal's eyes were starting to water. They stared at each other for a few moments, just letting the simple feel of one another's touch connect them.

"How'd you manage to find me anyway?" Anubis finally asked.

"I still have some magic left." Thoth said with a wink, "It took a good deal of searching, especially since you've crossed the great ocean to come to this land." He paused, and then added "I'd heard you'd been gone for some time and I wanted to check up on you, old friend." He punctuated that by brushing his fingers through the black fur on the back of Anubis' hand.

Anubis' expression brightened at that, his ears flicking up. Thoth's eyes were bright at finally having found him. He'd been worried about his old companion wandering alone in this strange new world. He'd also missed the moody jackal and was glad he'd get to spend some time with him again. There was another reason he'd searched him out though, one he wasn't going to mention just then. He'd wait until his compatriot was in a better frame of mind for that.

"Well thank-you for coming to look for me" Anubis replied, and grasped Thoth's hand in both of his.

"I have missed you, old friend... Would you settle for my company to keep you warm tonight?"

"Gladly, hon," the jackal god replied. He let his mouth hang open just slightly, showing a glimpse of his teeth. It was the first genuine smile he'd felt in longer than he cared to think about.

"So, should we retire to someplace better then?"

"Awww, you just got here, why don't we stay awhile and see some more of this new world's culture." Anubis' smile widened as he cocked his ear and added "perhaps I could even get you out on the dance floor..."

Thoth just shook his head again, but said nothing. The gleam in his eyes betrayed the warmth he felt growing in the chambers of his heart at seeing Anubis again. He was remembering the zeal the old jackal possessed, along with his moody disposition, and he could feel his old lover's excitement infecting him.

"Perhaps," he finally said. "Though if I'm going to accept that hospitality, I think more libations are in order" he added with another wink.

Anubis was all too happy to oblige. He was up in an instant and off to the bar, his tail swishing slightly behind him as he walked. It was good to see him happy again, and what did a little celebration hurt? Now that he'd found Anubis, there'd be time for more serious talk and planning later. Thoth realized he could use a little kick-back too; now that he thought about it, it had been some time for himself as well. The quest could wait until tomorrow.

6   Will A. Sanborn

Chapter 2: Welcome to the Jungle

There's a big dark town, it's a place I've found
There's a world going on underground
They're alive, they're awake
While the rest of the world is asleep
  Tom Waits, "Underground"

I woke up alarmed
I didn't know where I was at first
Just that I woke up in your arms
And almost immediately I felt sorry
  Liz Phair, "Fuck and Run"

The sound roused him from his sleep, and Thomas opened his eyes at the intrusion to his peaceful slumber. He blinked when he realized he wasn't in his hotel room. A moment later he figured out that he was in the gypsy's trailer. Not only that, but he was in the gypsy's bed, and even nestled against the warm body of the gypsy herself as she lay sleeping beside him. He took in the sight of the blue-skinned dragon's head peaking out from under the covers and the blurred memories from the night before started coming back to him.

He didn't have time for a reverie though, for a couple of seconds later there was a loud pounding on the door, followed by a man's voice "Ishandra, wake up, I've got to talk to you."

Whoever it was, the man sounded serious, and his business urgent; Thomas didn't like the sound of that. He sat up quickly, and in doing so he roused the sleeping reptile exotic next to him. She sputtered awake, and glanced up at him as she blinked the sleep from her eyes.

The knocking came again and she turned her attention to the door. "What is it, Mark?" she asked, her voice still groggy.

Without warning, the door opened, and Thomas was caught holding the bed covers against himself as a man walked in. The sight of him added to the shock. He was an older man, probably in his late 50's. His face showed signs of having lived a hard, wild life, and his eyes burned with intensity. His hair was in need of being cut, growing wild and tangled. It showed no signs of thinning, though the color was starting to fade. To complete the image, he had a chaotic tribal tattoo on the right side of his face, framing his eye and cheek.

The man took a look at Thomas and his expression abruptly changed, showing shock and surprise. He stared at Thomas for a moment, and then his look became that of humility as he turned towards the dragon gypsy. "I'm sorry, Ishandra, I didn't know you were entertaining anyone... I'll wait for you guys to get dressed, but I do need to talk with you. It's very important."

Thomas didn't like how insistent the man had sounded with that last part. Even though he'd left the bedroom and closed the door behind him, the young man knew that the stranger was just waiting in the next room. He did his best to gain his composure, but as he turned to look at his exotic lover, the scared confusion was written all across his face.

"Don't worry about him," came her reply to his wordless question. "That's just Mark, my husband."

"Your husband?" The words fell out of his mouth, mixed with a low gasp.

"Yes sweetie, it's okay" she said as she touched his arm to comfort him. "He knows all about this and we have it all worked out. He's not mad, just a little embarrassed at surprising us."

"Are you sure?"

"Of course, though it really must be something important for him to barge in like that." Thomas only stared at her as she continued. "I need to talk with him right away. So get dressed, but don't go anywhere. I really enjoyed last night and I want to have breakfast with you at least." She gave his arm a squeeze, showing her powers of persuasion, as she'd done the night before.

Thomas moved slowly as he got out of bed and found his clothes strewn along the floor. He felt as if he was still caught in dream as he remembered more of the events of the previous evening. Mixed emotions tugged at him. That certainly wasn't something he was used to doing. He stole a look at her body, seeing her back and tail, taking in the sight of her cobalt skin, and a couple of other feelings washed over him.

He finally managed to get out of his stupor and get dressed. She opened the door and ushered him out into the sitting room of her trailer, where the night before she'd offered to tell his fortune, before offering other things. Her husband now stood in that room, looking agitated, but not hostile. He even managed a friendly smile at Thomas as Ishandra made introductions."

"I'm awfully sorry about barging in on you like that," the older man said as he gripped the young man's hand firmly.

"That's okay" Thomas heard himself say as he looked into the face of the gypsy's spouse. And then Ishandra ushered him outside, reminding him again to stick around, that she wasn't finished with him yet.

Thomas' thoughts were clouded as he sat down on the steps to his trailer. What was he doing here? After all the wandering he'd done, he still didn't feel any closer to finding what he was looking for. He certainly felt more lost than usual after the events of last night. Why had it happened? He'd certainly never done something that rash before, but maybe the loneliness of the road was getting to him more than he realized. It was hard trying to find your way, and so far it'd been nothing like the voyage of discovery he'd planned. Drifting between odd jobs from city to city as he trekked cross country seemed every bit as futile as taking classes had been.

Will A. Sanborn

The carnival had seemed an interesting stop at first, a chance to see how the other half lived. He'd never seen a real live freak show before, and it had lived up to its promise to amaze and disturb him. That'd probably only added to the feeling of isolation though, so when Ishandra had approached him later on, he'd been open to talking to her. She'd settled his wariness and put him at ease, and had even invited him back to her trailer for a psychic reading. She hadn't told him anything he didn't already know, and had made a few lucky guesses about his background, but otherwise that endeavor had been pretty pointless.

It had got them talking though, and perhaps it was just any port in the storm for him, after driving so many miles alone, but he'd felt a connection with her. Then again maybe it was just hormones and natural curiosity. Having someone give you attention can be intoxicating, especially after spending so much time alone, only listening to your thoughts. It probably didn't hurt that she was an exotic, an attractive and mysterious one at that. Even among the exotics, reptiles were a small minority.

He smiled a little as he thought of her in that way. No matter what else he felt, he couldn't deny that it had been a memorable evening and a rewarding one at that. Even with how quick things had progressed, it had felt good to couple with her. He felt himself blush slightly at the thought of taking a lover so quickly. He chided himself that he didn't even know the first thing about her, such as her having a husband, for instance. That thought jumped out at him, surfacing to the top of his consciousness after he'd tried so hard not to think around it. He felt a dull gnawing in pit of his stomach as he remembered the look on Mark's face when he'd burst in on them and he felt like a fool all over again. Even if what they said was true, that he was truly okay with it, did it really make things alright? It didn't help him feel any better.

He felt the impulse to leave again; to get up off those steps and walk briskly away, not turning around, not saying good-bye. He could make it to his car, then be on the road and never look back. But off to where? That was the question. He didn't feel like driving any more just then. Plus, Ishandra's insistent plea for him to stay around, so they could talk some more, kept on pulling at him. It helped to offset the other thoughts nipping away at him. So, for lack of anything better to do, he stayed and waited. He was good at waiting things out.

He tried to distract himself from the thoughts at hand, so instead of gazing down at his shoes while his mind wrapped around itself, he looked up and checked out his surroundings. Things looked different now that the sun was out. He hadn't gotten a good look at the landscape when they'd come here the night before. It had already been dark for a couple of hours once she'd offered to take him back to her place, and while there had been colored circus lights all around, it had only lit things up partway.

This morning the bright sun cast a different look at the place. It still had a carnival atmosphere, but not quite the dream-like mood from the night before. It still managed to be surreal enough though. As he looked about from his vantage point on the gypsy's steps, he could see all the citizens of this little community starting about their daily business. It was perhaps just like any other small town, with people moving about, tending to their own matters, but there were obvious differences. For starters the feel of the place was definitely transient. All the structures were trailers, trucks or tents, and while they were set up as neatly as possible, the order was not perfect. There were setups for utilities strung between the settlements, lines for power and hoses for water.

What made things even more distinctive though were the members of this special community themselves. Never before had Thomas seen such a high percentage of exotics among the crowd, not to mention the freaks. Of course it was a perfect environment for the latter, one of the places they could feel at home and be celebrated instead of shunned. Some exotics from small towns might find the atmosphere inviting as well, especially those with any interest in show business.

As he watched, a couple caught his eye. A female exotic, a white tiger, was walking along with a severely-deformed man. He had lumps on his face, with one of the bulges encroaching on his eye. His left arm was shrunken and withered, and he walked with a slight limp. As the two of them walked along, talking as friends and peers, he noticed the freak looked perfectly at ease; even the imperfection in his step didn't seem to be adversely affecting him. Thomas tried not to look too closely, but his curiosity got the better of him. A moment later they caught his gaze and waved at him. He managed a smile and a little wave of his own, and was thankful that they paid him little heed. He was in their world now, just part of the scenery.

"Well, hello there" a voice next to him rang out, startling him from his reverie.

He flinched, and then turned to look at whoever had addressed him. Unsure of what to expect, he was even more surprised when he had to drop his gaze downward to meet the mysterious stranger who'd addressed him. There before him stood a midget smiling up at him. Even though he was seated, Thomas was still about a half a foot taller than him. That was partially due to him sitting on the top of the stairs, but also due to the very short stature of the little man who stood before him.

At the same time Thomas registered the presence of another person, someone taller, taller than both of them in fact. Standing off to the side and behind the midget was a tall gangly man. He was at least six feet, and probably several inches over that. He was bald, his scalp not looking shaved, but naturally denuded of hair. Even the man's eyebrows were thin. What's more his skin was a dark green, which was probably another by-product of genetics, not cosmetics. The lean tall man was smiling at him as well, but his mouth was open leaving his teeth visible. They'd been filed down to points, which offset the congenial impression he was going for.

Thomas flinched in spite of himself, and then struggled to keep his composure. The midget just laughed at that, but his laughter was warm and

Will A. Sanborn

inviting. He offered his squat arm to Thomas, and Thomas found himself shaking hands with the diminutive man.

"I'm sorry to startle you," the midget said. His voice was a slightly higher pitch than normal, and his words came out soft and warm. "We saw you sitting there, looking a little lost and thought we'd introduce ourselves." He paused, and then added, "I'm Jeremy, and this is The Geek. He can't speak much, but he's a nice friend to have around." As he said that, Jeremy glanced up at the midget's giant companion and gave him a warm smile. The green man grinned down at him with warm admiration.

"Uh, I'm Thomas" the young man said, now feeling even more like an outsider. He paused briefly, searching for something more to say, then added "it's nice to meet you guys."

"You a friend of Ishandra's?" Jeremy asked.

Thomas nodded dully, "yeah." He felt like adding that he'd just met her, but that didn't seem necessary to reveal.

"Is everything okay, you look a little worried?" The midget gave him an earnest look, his eyes reflecting genuine concern.

Jeremy's voice was so low that for a moment Thomas got a quick impression of talking to a young child. That faded just as quickly though as he saw the stubble on the midget's chin. "I guess so... They're just inside talking, something important came up, but she wants to talk with me afterwards..." As soon as he'd said it he felt his face heating up at having said too much.

"Oh yeah, the preacher, we heard he came home early. He got in this morning all excited about something. Thali said he'd seemed in a hurry when he'd passed her near the gates." Reading Thomas' expression, Jeremy was quick to add "oh, don't worry about Mark, that wasn't about you, I can assure you of that. If he had a problem with you, you'd know about it already."

That strange assurance didn't do anything to make Thomas feel any better. He still didn't like the idea of Ishandra's husband being so worked up about something, not to mention the fact that she had a husband to begin with.

Noting Thomas' discomfort, Jeremy shifted the conversation. "Ishandra's very nice, isn't she?"

That didn't help matters all that much, but Thomas did have to agree with the midget that yes, the dragon gypsy was quite nice. He blushed again as he voiced that affirmation, but Jeremy just ignored it and gave him another smile.

"Yeah, she's a real piece of work. She can be pretty persuasive if she wants to be, but she's got a heart of gold. She's not really my type, but I don't mind looking. She's a real fun tease too." Getting only nods from Thomas at this, Jeremy added "you're lucky that she took a fancy to you. When she likes you that much that means she thinks you're something special."

"Well thanks" Thomas said; it was the only semi-intelligent reply he could think of making.

"Hey, if Ishandra likes you, then you're good in my book, Thomas... It's nice meeting you but we should be going to get breakfast. I'd invite you along, but I'm sure Ishandra and Mark will get you something."

"Okay, thanks anyways."

"No problem. You take care and maybe we'll see you around."

Thomas nodded again and with that they were off. Jeremy shook his hand again and then as they were leaving, the Geek grunted something to him and smiled again. Thomas was alone on the steps as he watched the two mismatched friends walking away. He was left with his thoughts once again.

He wondered what it meant that Jeremy had said they might see him around again. Could it be possible that he'd end up stopping here awhile? It was true that he didn't really have any place in particular to be, but how was he going to fit in at the carnival? That seemed like the last place he'd end up.

'Gooble gobble. One of us... One of us...' He pushed that thought down. No, that didn't seem to fit at all.

He wasn't left alone with his thoughts for too much longer though. He soon heard the door to the trailer open behind him. Turning around he saw Ishandra looking down at him.

"Come on in, Thomas" she said; her voice was just as sweet as ever. "Let's get some breakfast."

Will A. Sanborn

Will A. Sanborn

Chapter 3: Going Down the Rabbit Hole

We sometimes catch a window, a glimpse of what's beyond
Was it just imagination, stringing us along?
More things than are dreamed about, unseen and unexplained
We suspend our disbelief, and we are entertained
  Rush, "Mystic Rhythms"

But when I look into your eyes you don't believe me
I can see it in your eyes you don't believe
  Alan Parsons Project, "You Don't Believe"

Ishandra watched Thomas carefully as he sipped at the cup of coffee she'd given him. He noticed that Mark was watching him too, not as intently, but still with some interest, and maybe a little concern. At least the older man didn't seem to harbor any ill-will towards him, so that put him a little at ease. He still didn't feel all that comfortable sharing breakfast with this couple, one half of whom he'd spent the previous evening with. It didn't seem to matter to him that he hadn't known she was involved with anyone. Hell, it still felt odd that he'd gone to bed with her in the first place. He didn't feel any less uneasy from the talk he'd just had with the midget Jeremy either, he maybe felt even more unsure because of it. He didn't belong here.

Ishandra finally broke the silence. "You're still uncertain about last night, aren't you Thomas?"

He nodded dully and managed to give a curt reply. "Yes."

"You don't regret it do you? I thought we had fun, you had a good time, right?"

He glanced from her to Mark's face before answering. The man was still watching him, but he looked mostly disinterested. He didn't seem concerned about them talking about their carnal exploits in front of him. He seemed more impatient to talk about something he considered more important. Thomas wasn't sure if he wanted to find out what that was. He was still half regretting sticking around, even though the lovely dragon had asked him to. He caught himself thinking that. Even with the mix of emotions he felt sitting between this very strange couple, he couldn't deny there was an attraction he felt for her.

"No, it's not that," he finally answered her. "It was very nice being with you." He half regretted saying that, feeling foolish at admitting that while her husband could hear him. He paused, trying to collect his thoughts. "It's just that I've never done that before... no I mean with someone I'd just met." She smiled slightly at that, but didn't say anything. The look she gave him felt like she wanted more, and soon he heard it being dragged out of him. "I've never been with an exotic before either..."

Then he felt really stupid. He might not be an ivy-league graduate, he wasn't even a student any more, but that didn't mean he was some ignorant rube. He didn't like the way his last confession made him sound so dumb. He dropped his eyes from her face. He kept from looking at Mark as well.

"Shhhh hon, don't worry about it." He felt her take his hand, while her other hand reached out to cup his chin. She lifted his head with gentle insistence, until his gaze met hers once again. "I had a feeling that was the case, it's nothing to be ashamed about."

"I'm sorry it came out that way, Ishandra. I know it didn't sound that flattering."

"Not at all, Thomas. Eloquence is not always required. I asked you for how you felt and you answered truthfully. Now would you feel any better if I was a human woman?"

He shook his head, but still kept focus on her gaze. He couldn't turn away from those green eyes which were looking at him with a warm intensity. "No, it probably wouldn't change things that much..."

"I know you're worried about Mark, hon and that was a bit of surprise. I didn't expect him back so early this morning, but it's better he did come while you were still here, no matter how uncomfortable it makes you feel."

Thomas didn't know how to respond to that, so he stayed silent and let her continue. "I want to tell you again not to worry about that though. Mark and I have an understanding. We've had this agreement for a long time, and it's how things work for us."

"And I want you to know I hold no ill-will against you Thomas" Mark added. The young man felt a shiver run down his spine as her husband finally spoke. "Again I'm sorry for bursting in on you this morning. I should've been thinking more... I'd feel more embarrassed about it if things weren't so important."

Thomas still felt as if his head was stuffed with cotton. His mind was still sluggish as it tried to wrap around everything that'd happened that morning. He did manage to turn his attention, however briefly, towards Mark. He even took the hand the man was offering him and made an effort to shake it, even if he was only going through the motions. Mark met his loose grip with a very firm one. For a second Thomas was afraid the man might try and crush his hand, but then he realized that Mark's handshake was just as serious as the rest of him.

"There, that wasn't so bad was it, hon?" Ishandra asked, drawing his attention back to her after Mark had released his hand. "I know this is a lot for you to take in, but it's important we get over this. I knew last night when I was reading you that you were something special, but after talking with Mark, I think you might be even more than that."

Thomas felt another shiver ripple through him. "I don't understand" he said, hearing how hollow his voice sounded. "I don't even know what I'm doing here, how this even happened..."

Will A. Sanborn

"You think I took advantage of you, don't you?" Ishandra asked, and he could feel the intensity of her gaze on him yet again. Those eyes were so expressive, but they showed great care for him.

"I don't know, I've never felt like this... I don't know if I've felt that way last night either." As he spoke those words, a thought ran through him, a flicker of memory flashing up from his subconscious. "That drink, you put something in it, didn't you?"

She chuckled at that. "No, it was just regular alcohol. I trust you're used to that, anyone your age should be used to that, especially someone who's been to college." He felt a sting from those words, but realized she hadn't meant it that way, or maybe she had. She did know that part of his history at least. "I may have seduced you, but you were in complete possession of you faculties while I did it."

He stared back at her blackly. Seduced him, but how? All she'd done is worked on his reading, given him a half-assed fortune, something about him finding his way, that a change was coming, something for the better. It'd sounded like the standard shtick and he hadn't paid much attention to it. Then she'd offered him a glass of wine, and he'd decided to drink it, even though it should've been against his better judgment. Even then things didn't seem too odd. He tried to remember it back, but things seemed a little hazy. If he could recall correctly, he thought he'd made the first moves, resting his hand on her arm as he was asking her about her life in the carnival.

She smiled at his puzzled look. "It was just a simple spell, hon, more of a charm really? No, don't be shocked, it wasn't anything drastic. I'd never do anything to someone I didn't want happening to me, 'return thrice fold' as they say. No, it was only a little push to get you to act on your inner feelings. I sensed you were interested in me, even when I'd met you on the midway and invited you back here. If you had no feelings for me then nothing would've happened. The charm wouldn't make you do anything you didn't really want to do anyway..." She gave his arm a suggestive squeeze as she added the last part.

"But why? Why me, why go after someone random at all?"

"Well first because I thought you were cute." He felt himself blush at that comment, even in spite of himself. Again he chanced a glance at Mark, who was smiling slightly, but still looking impatient.

"You also looked a little lost out there, and I thought I might be able to help you in some way. I'd planned on talking with you more this morning... You also felt like someone who was curious, who was open to possibilities, but might not realize it or even admit it to themselves."

He shook his head at that; he didn't feel that way at all.

"Oh really, then why'd you bother to check out the carnival at all? It's not the sort of thing your average person does, especially alone. It's more of a dating activity for someone your age isn't it?"

"So you figured I'd be an easy target then?" Thomas was reminded again that she was an exotic, and a reptilian one at that. He remembered how some exotics tried to distance themselves from humans, finding themselves more akin to their distant animal counterparts. Could she really be a dragon-lady? She didn't seem cold at all. She'd certainly been warm and inviting last night... He caught himself thinking that and felt his face heat up again in another blush.

"No, not at all, Thomas. You've got to try and trust me when I say that I found you interesting and could see that you were lonely and thought this might be good for you... I enjoyed it a lot myself too. You're an eager lover."

She paused and they looked at each other for a few moments; the silence weighed heavy between them. He just didn't know what to say, he hardly knew what to feel about it. She was right about how it had been good for him at the time though.

Finally she spoke again. "Do you think you can leave it at that for now?" she asked him. "I know you're still unsure, but we've got other things to discuss."

"Okay" he said, his voice still low, but he felt himself rise to her challenge. She seemed to care about him enough to keep him around this morning, so he could stick around and see where things went. As she'd suggested, he really didn't have anywhere else to be just then, and no matter how weird the morning was turning out to be, he had to admit he was at least a little curious as to what this was all about. At thinking that he worried that she might have charmed him yet again, but he forced that thought down. If he double-guessed everything he'd just make it worse.

"Good, it's about time" he heard Mark say. The man's voice was tinged with a hint of annoyance.

"Mark, remember your hospitality" Ishandra said to him, her voice serious, but sounding caring too.

"I'm sorry" he said, nodding to her, and then turned to look at Thomas. "I didn't mean anything by it son, it's just that even after all these years I can still be gruff sometimes... I know it's important what you guys were talking about, but with what I've been itching to say, it's been hard to sit still."

Thomas felt the lump in his throat return as he heard Mark mention that, but as he looked at the man, he still didn't show any resentment. Instead he looked almost like a kid who was bristling with excitement to tell his friends some important secret and could barely contain it any longer.

"Okay dear," Ishandra said to him. I'll put some more coffee on and you can start your story."

Ishandra got up to tend to the coffee pot and Thomas switched his attention to Mark, still feeling unsure as to what exactly was going on. Mark just looked at him for a couple of moments, perhaps studying him, or maybe just searching for the right words to say. The room grew quiet, as Thomas waited for the older man to speak.

Finally Mark began. "Okay son, I know you're going to have a hard time believing this, so just let me get finished with all of it before you say anything, okay?" Thomas gave a silent nod and Mark continued. "I was out exploring the area. I go out for drives sometimes, just to get away and see what's around. I

Will A. Sanborn

usually plan on being gone for a couple of days, but what happened last night changed that." After a brief pause, Mark added "I was out driving on one of the back roads when I saw the angel again..."

'The angel?' Thomas thought and blinked his eyes as he stared back at Mark. He then turned his head to look back at Ishandra, who nodded in agreement and motioned for him to turn back around.

"Now stay with me here, I know it sounds crazy, but you need to listen to it all." He was watching Thomas intently now. "Yes, I saw an angel, the same one I've seen before. She saved my life once, years ago... She was there, just standing along the side of the road, waiting for me. I know well enough now not to disregard a message from above, so I pulled over. She got in my truck and we had a long talk."

Thomas glanced sideways. He noted that Ishandra was still behind him and gauged the distance to the door. Neither Mark nor Ishandra looked crazy, but he didn't like how this was sounding. If Mark noticed his unease, he didn't mention it to Thomas, instead he continued with his tale. "I don't know if you're a religious man son, but I tell you that the angels do exist and they come down here sometimes to do God's work. Sometimes they even enlist others to help them out. Now ever since that angel saved my life, I've been paying back a debt, and trying to do what He'd ask of me... Last night the angel told me that we're all in danger."

"Danger?" Thomas asked. His mouth felt dry as he parted his lips to speak. "What kind of danger?"

"It could be the end of everything."

"You mean Armageddon, the end of the world?" Thomas' voice belayed his disbelief, but again Mark ignored it.

"Yes, something's coming that could end it all, and it's up to us to stop it?"

"What do you mean 'us'?"

"Well, Ishandra and myself, and I think you?"

"No, that doesn't make any sense, why you two, and what about me? You just met me." Thomas heard his voice becoming louder as he offered his challenge.

"Well, myself, I've been touched by the power of God, and Ishandra, she has her own qualifications which I'll let her explain. As for you, I didn't know it would be you at the time. All the angel said is that we'd meet someone new, someone young and inexperienced, but open to possibilities. She said that we needed to get you come along with us, that you were needed to stop the threat. Then when I got back and found you here, and talked with Ishandra about what she thought about you, we both agreed that you're the likely candidate."

Thomas shook his head. His mind felt stuffed up again, like it had earlier. He turned to look at Ishandra for support; surely she couldn't be going along with this. She was beside him a moment later and placed a hand on his shoulder as he looked up at her. "I know it's got to be hard to take Thomas, but from what Mark's told me, I think he's right, that you are the person we need.

Sometimes things happen for a reason, and I think it was no accident that I met you last night." She paused, and then added "I was serious when I said I thought you were someone special, I got that feeling when I did that reading on you."

"Okay, that's it!" Thomas exclaimed in frustration. "I don't know what game you guys are playing, but I don't want to be a part of it. Maybe you think it's funny to play around with me, to see how much fun you can have with your new playmate, but I've heard enough."

He made an effort to stand up, but Ishandra pushed against him, holding him down against the chair. A shudder ran through him as he realized the strength she was able to muster, which she'd kept hidden before.

"No Thomas, we're serious," she said, her voice still soft, but her eyes looking at him intently.

Thomas stopped fighting her and searched his mind for something to say to her. "Okay Ishandra, let's talk about that reading you did for me then. If you were able to sense so much about me, how come I wasn't amazed by what you said? Everything I heard sounded pretty run of the mill to me." He realized that perhaps it wasn't the best idea to argue with her over her supposed abilities, but he was desperate and the only option he could see was to try and use logic to diffuse the situation.

"I read that you'd gone to college but hadn't finished" came her reply; her voice was cool and collected.

"That's not really a big deal, Ishandra. You yourself said that it was strange for a person my age to be around here. You probably just figured out I was a drop-out who was trying to find myself. Everything else you said could've just been some clever social engineering. It's just show-biz anyway..."

He saw her eyes go wide, and felt her grip tighten on his shoulder, if only for a moment. "So you don't believe me at all then, Thomas?"

He shook his head, "no, I'm sorry Ishandra, but I can't."

"Very well then" she said as she took a seat next to him, leaving one hand still on his shoulder. Her voice was still low, but insistent. "Give me your hand."

"What?"

"Give me your hand. If you didn't believe the reading I did last night, then I'll do another one for you. I didn't tell you everything I felt last night, and now that I know you better I can get deeper."

When he hesitated, she reached out and took his hand, placing it in her firm grasp. Thomas looked over at Mark who was still sitting across the table from him. He looked impatient again, but not hostile.

Ishandra stared at him. "So you want proof, then I'll give you something out of a memory that I couldn't possibly know." Thomas watched her faced in disbelief. Her brilliant green eyes drew his attention as he looked into her intense gaze. As his eyes focused in on hers, he caught the subtle movement of her pupils. As he watched they expanded and contracted ever so slightly, fluctuating as if in time with her heartbeat.

Will A. Sanborn

They stayed like that as the seconds ticked out between them. Finally she broke the silence. "Your cousin, he was about your age."

He paused, digging through his memory for the name. "Fred, what about him?"

"One summer when you were in your early teens your parents drove cross-country to see relatives and you spent a week at your cousin Fred's house."

"So," he asked, as an old memory resurfaced. He didn't like where this might be going, but tried to keep his composure.

"He talked you into playing strip poker, and eventually you had your first sexual experience. It wasn't anything big, but you watched each other get off. You did it a couple more times too. It was exciting and forbidden, but later you felt guilty about it."

He paused and stared at her, his mouth open. "It was just something I did as kid..." he said. A moment later he added "why the hell did you have to bring that up?"

"You don't need to be embarrassed Thomas, it was completely natural."

He felt his face heating up again. He pulled his hand from her grasp and turned away from her. He couldn't help but glance over at Mark though. He saw the older man was smirking, but when Thomas met his eyes, Mark's expression paled slightly. Thomas grabbed the table tightly with his hand, holding onto it as he fought his embarrassment.

It was then when the full gravity of the situation hit him. "Ishandra" he said as he looked up, daring to face her again, "how'd you know that, can you really read minds? You're a telepath?!"

"Not quite, hon, more like an empath. I can mainly read emotions and memories, if I try hard. I'm sorry I brought that up. I was just looking for something good, with a strong emotion with it that would show you what I could do. That was one of the stronger ones that I found with just a quick look."

"But it happened so long ago."

"It still had a strong emotion attached to it, even if you hadn't recalled it in years. It was the best impression I got from you that would prove my abilities were real."

"Can you see the future too?"

"Sometimes, but then it's usually still pretty hazy. Divination is much more difficult, and unpredictable. Even in the old days seeing the flow of time and eventualities could be random, and it's much harder now." She sounded sad as she spoke the last part, but that emotion was fleeting. "There's something else you need to see Thomas, to help you believe." She turned to her husband and held out her hand. "Mark can I see your knife?"

Thomas pushed back from her as she took the knife from the older man; that time she did not try and stop him though. He watched her and held his breath as she removed the blade from its sheath in a casual manner, and he waited to see what she was going to do. She surprised him by bringing the knife to her other hand and with a quick motion she sliced the blade deep into her palm.

Thomas heard his gasp as her crimson blood spilled from the wound to pour across her blue skin. He saw her grimace slightly, but she made no move to stop the flow. She reached out for a napkin instead, to catch the blood as it fell from her injured palm. Then, as he watched, the flow of blood eased off, and within moments stopped all together. A few seconds later she used the bloody napkin to clean off her hand, then held it up to him. Besides the dark red smear on her palm, her flesh was unmarred. The wound had completely vanished; there wasn't even a scar there, where less than a minute before there'd been a gaping wound.

"I know that wasn't the best of ways to show you that either, Thomas, but it got the point across as well. I trust that will help you believe that there's magic in the world, behind the scenes of what you see everyday?"

"But how?" he managed to ask her.

"I'm not the regular exotic you think I am," she replied as she cleaned the blade of the knife with the napkin and then licked the remaining traces of blood off of her hand.

"What, what do you mean, Ishandra?"

"I'm an immortal, Thomas. I've been here a long time, a lot longer than you could guess." Again there was a momentary flash of sadness in her eyes.

"So what, are you some kind of god?"

"Goddess hon," she corrected him. The light in her eyes returned and a hint of a smile began to spread across her muzzle. "I'm not the goddess, but I am of her."

Thomas was shaking his head when he heard Mark say "It's kind of like the Trinity. It can be hard to wrap your mind around it if you think about it too hard."

Ishandra nodded to her husband. "Yes. The goddess of my people wanted to be closer to us, so she shared her essence with a priestess. The priestess became pregnant and gave birth to a special child. That child was me, the goddess incarnated in the flesh, made immortal. I was way the goddess could commune with her people, and I served that role for centuries."

"So, how'd you end up here?" Thomas regretted his bluntness as soon as he'd said it, but she paid it no mind.

"The goddess is eternal, Thomas, but her dominion was not. As all empires tend to do, ours fell. Our religion died out, to be replaced by other gods. As the followers dwindled, the goddess' powers over this world faded as well. That is why I can't do as much as I once could..."

"I'm sorry Ishandra, I didn't know" Thomas said and instinctively reached out for her hand, even before he knew what he was doing. "You must miss her."

She gave him a slow nod. "I can still feel my connection with her, but it is more of a whisper now." She paused as she squeezed his hand and forced a

Will A. Sanborn

smile for him. "That is the way of the world though. I have seen civilizations rise and fall as I've watched this world change. It was my destiny to experience this life, and I have taken the world as I've found it. The journey continues."

"So now do you believe that what I said is possible?" Mark asked.

"I suppose so," Thomas answered after a slight hesitation. His mind still felt numb with it all, but for the moment the best he could do was go along with it. "So I can see that you've been chosen by an angel, and Ishandra as well because of the way she is, but what does this have to do with me?"

"I really don't know son, the angel wasn't all that specific. It just seems that from what she said, you fit the bill."

"But what are we even going up against, and why is it up to us to save the world?" Even as he was saying it, Thomas couldn't believe his own words.

"That's the nature of God. From what I've observed he doesn't like to show his hand openly all that much. He'd rather work through indirect means, which this time means us. I don't know much more than I've already told you. The angel said that we're to head east. I imagine we'll learn more as we're making the journey, when we're ready for it."

"So you're just going on blind faith?"

"Faith, but it's not blind. I know you can't understand why I feel this way, but I trust whatever message God sends me, and I'll do His will." Mark paused as he looked at Thomas. The intensity was back in his eyes, but they showed an earnest need as well. "Will you come along with us, Thomas?"

Thomas shook his head slowly. "I don't know. I need some breathing room to think this over." He made as to stand up and felt his balance waiver. "On second thought, I think I need to lie down."

Will A. Sanborn

Chapter 4: Good Morning, There's Something You Should Know

I rode a western wind with a girl over to her mother's
In the backyard stars shone brighter than the others
That I rarely see through the smog through the haze that covers
The home that I used to live in

Well I kind of sort of knew what was going to happen
When she put her number down on a restaurant napkin
She said goodbye, I think the words were
When you're back in town let's have each other again
I'll come around and see you again

Like Jessica Rabbit she collects bad habits, gets her drinks for free
Animated vixen stole Cupid's arrow and came to rescue me
In the blink of an eyelid my lid opened up and I could see
That she'd come to rescue me
      Eve 6, "Rescue"

Thoth awoke slowly, gradually becoming aware of his surroundings. Traces of the morning's light were filtering in from behind the curtains which were drawn across the window of the hotel room. There was enough light getting in to let him see things clearly though. He thought about getting up, but feeling the warmth of Anubis sleeping beside him, he delayed that action.

It had been awhile since he'd taken a lover; his passions didn't usually run that high, and certainly not as hot as Anubis' did. Still, it was nice to spend an evening with an old friend and lover again. He certainly wasn't dead in his loins, and after fasting, it was nice to have an occasional feast. He absently let out a contented sigh as his thoughts returned to the night before. He and Anubis had both helped each other remember old times, and for a brief passage, even relive them to a point. He leaned his head gently against the sleeping jackal's shoulder. He closed his eyes slightly and breathed in, catching the low scent of his lover. He could wait awhile to get up. For the moment it just felt nice to live in the present.

Moments passed, perhaps they were minutes, he wasn't keeping count, but then he gradually felt his companion stirring. Anubis was just as leisurely at waking as Thoth had been. With his eyes still closed the jackal's hands navigated their way to find the ibis' warmth and curl around his body. Thoth's arm did the same, working almost of its own accord, and draped itself over Anubis' side, resting at the small of his back. Thoth heard both their breathing in his ear as he lost himself in the jackal's warmth.

It wasn't until he felt the tongue giving his cheek a gentle lick that he opened his eyes. Anubis pulled his head back slightly and Thoth was greeted by those large, expressive, yellow eyes staring up at him. The avian couldn't help but winking his eye as he gazed back at Anubis. Even with everything that'd been on his mind of late, Thoth felt his cares drifting to the back of his mind once again, just like they had the previous evening. There were times when the jackal's emotions could be so infectious, and this was morning was another one of them.

Anubis didn't say anything, he just held his lover close as he gently squeezed his body against Thoth's. Thoth felt his breath escape him; it made a low sound, slightly more audible than normal. He closed his eyes again and took another breath. He caught another whiff of the jackal's scent and absently-mindedly noted that it was getting stronger, and its characteristics changing too.

He felt Anubis' warm breath blow on his neck, and a moment later he felt his lover's leg move with gentle insistence between the two of his. The jackal further demonstrated his intentions by running his fingers through the fine mesh of feathers which covered Thoth's body. Those fingers continued to caress him through the soft downy covering, ambling on their way to their intended target. Finally, after several teasing moments, Thoth felt one of jackal's hands come to rest on his lower back, the other one brushing ever so gently along the contour of his crotch.

With his eyes still closed, the ibis submitted to his friend's ardor. He parted his legs and opened his loins to his lover. A moment later he felt those tender fingers touching him, and sparks of pleasure fueled his growing desire. He heard his own voice give a low moan, and as Anubis took his flesh in a loving grasp, the jackal gave his own sigh of emphatic approval.

◆ ◆ ◆

Thoth emerged from the bathroom after his shower to the scent of fresh-brewed coffee. Anubis was dressed in a bathrobe and he motioned for his newly-reacquainted lover to sit down next to him on the couch. The jackal offered the ibis a bagel from the continental-breakfast selection in the kitchenette and then poured him a cup of coffee. Thoth accepted both, nodding in thanks to Anubis.

Anubis leaned against him on the couch, paying no mind to the how the ibis' feathers were still damp from the shower. In fact the jackal's hand soon found its way to Thoth's chest, his fingers casually stroking him there. His attentions were no longer erotic or insistent, now he was simply taking pleasure in his old friend's company.

"It's good to be with you again Thoth," Anubis said as he looked at him. "It reminds me a little of old times. I miss working together with you..." The jackal's ears dropped slightly at that, as he remembered the current state of the world. He then added "thanks for coming to find me, hon. That means a lot to me."

Thoth felt the slightest twinge of guilt trickle through him. "It's good to see you again too, Anubis" he said as he put his breakfast aside for the moment and brought one hand to rest on the jackal's leg, offering comfort and reassurance. He paused, and then added "I do really care about you, and it warms my heart to see how I can ease your loneliness... However, Anubis, I need to tell you that it wasn't the only reason I came to seek you out."

Anubis cocked his head to the side, his face showing confusion and a slight hurt. He said nothing, only continued to look at his companion. Thoth looked back at him, waiting a moment, then continued. "It's not as if I don't care about you Anubis, you know that. If you'd been out here long enough, I would've come looking for you anyway, to see how you were doing... It's just that something has come up, something that could be very important."

Anubis waited for him to continue. "Even though my magic has faded, I'm still sensitive to the remnants of magic that are left in the world." The jackal gave a solemn nod to that. "There's something happening, Anubis" Thoth added. "I'm not sure what it is, but there's definitely been an increase in the amount of energy lately."

"One of the new gods?" The jackal asked, as one of his ears turned back just the slightest bit.

"No, it doesn't feel like that. You know how the new gods don't like to make their presence known too greatly. They like to operate more subtly. Anyway, the presence I'm detecting is not like the spikes of one of their occasional miracles. It's more of a steady growth, slow for now, but getting more pronounced."

"So you don't have any idea what it is?"

"Not really," Thoth replied, shaking his head slightly. "It might not be anything to worry about... I know it's not our job to watch such things anymore, but like you, I still care about this world of the living, and I scry out over it occasionally."

"So you came out here to investigate?" Anubis asked; his voice still sounded a little incredulous.

"Yes, I'm curious. I haven't had a good mystery to solve in ages, and I figured now was as good a time as any to see what the world was like for this age." He gave Anubis' leg a playful squeeze and added "plus, it made for a good excuse to see you, old friend."

Anubis met Thoth's wink with a smile and flicked his ear at the ibis. "You can't fool me hon, you may not be as hot-blooded as I am, but it's okay to say you missed me... You certainly acted that way in bed."

They joined together in a chuckle over that, but Anubis broke the mood a few moments later when he looked at Thoth and his expression turned grave. "You don't think this new effect poses any danger, do you?"

"I don't know, it's still too far away to tell. I'm getting a better sense of it as I get closer, but I can't be certain of anything just yet. I do know it's an upset to the balance of things, and that has the potential for chaos and trouble."

"So you wanted me to help you check it out?"

"Yes, old friend. You were all ready out here, plus I too sometimes miss the old days of working along side you. If nothing else it'll give us both company for awhile, and if it does turn out to be something important, having someone to help me out could be good."

"I love you too, sweetie" Anubis replied, lightening the mood once again as he placed a hand on Thoth's cheek. "It does sound interesting and like something worthwhile to check out." His voice betrayed a little bit of his concern, but both of them chose to ignore that, at least for the moment.

Will A. Sanborn

Will A. Sanborn

Chapter 5: On the Road Again

On the road again
Like a band of gypsies we go down the highway
We're the best of friends
Insisting that the world be turnin' our way
And our way is on the road again
    Willie Nelson, "On the Road Again"

Every new beginning is a delicate time
But just like when the end comes, it's never very pretty
And every in-between time looks like a perfect picture
It seems to last forever, because it's standing still
    Devo, "A Change is Gonna Cum"

Thomas awoke in Ishandra's bed for the second time that day. This time he was allowed to come back into consciousness at a leisurely pace though, which was a great improvement over that morning. He laid there, blinking the sleep from his eyes as the memories of the day's events returned to him. It'd all been so much to take, that he'd needed to lie down. They'd helped him to her bed and had left him alone to rest. Before he'd known it, he'd fallen asleep, giving his tired mind a break. But now that he'd returned to the land of the living, he needed to sort out his thoughts.

It all seemed surreal to him, as if he still might be dreaming. He lay there, thinking of how he'd learned that Ishandra was some kind of ancient goddess, or something close. Even though her powers had faded over time, that still made him nervous. She'd been much easier to take as an exotic pretending to be a fortune teller. And then there was Mark with his orders from the heavenly messenger. It might have been easier if he'd been upset about catching them together, instead of being concerned with the quest which had been thrust upon them. And once more he realized that it looked like he was to be included as a member of that mission.

He still didn't believe that it really had anything to do with him. Part of his mind still questioned the validity of it. He would've questioned their sanity, and perhaps even his as well, if the proof Ishandra had showed him hadn't made such an impact. He'd been close enough the see her slice open her hand. The knife and the blood had been real, as well as the wound, which had torn open to reveal glistening red sinew. He shuddered as he thought about it again. He closed his eyes almost involuntary and he could see the event replaying itself from his memory. He saw the blood flowing from the savage wound, then drying up as her flesh had knit itself back together with seamless precision.

Whatever Ishandra was, she was more than just a regular exotic, much more, and that meant that what she was saying could very well be true. That in turn gave credence to Mark's tale, and the more he thought about it, the higher the house of cards built itself. No matter how incredulous it all seemed, he couldn't find the logic to fight against it. He sighed and felt trapped by the weight of that knowledge.

So what did that mean then? If Mark had talked to an angel, and she had told him about the impending danger, was it his problem? Just because they believed he was the one the angel had mentioned, even though her directions had been sufficiently vague, was he committed to going along with them? And what was the nature of this unknown threat? He didn't like the idea of chasing after something so obscure and not knowing what kind of perils might befall them.

He could of course try and walk away from this. He didn't think Mark and Ishandra would force him to come along with them, they didn't seem like they were that type of people. He didn't know how zealous Mark would be in following this cause though. Even without the uncertain pressure he might expect from them, other concerns pressed down upon him. Was it just a coincidence that he'd met Ishandra, and come back to spend the night with her to be thrust into this situation? The magic that Ishandra had showed him could very well go deeper than she was saying. It opened all sorts of possibilities that he didn't want to think about. If God, or Fate, or the Universe or whatever you wanted to call it wanted him to play along with His plans, he might not be able to ignore it. A random thought from his childhood bible lessons jumped out at him as he remembered the story of Jonah and the whale. Who knew what could happen to him if he tried to walk away from this now. He felt a shiver run through him as he pondered his options, which could very well be dwindling. A moment later he gritted his teeth. He didn't want to feel like a pawn in whatever game was going on here.

Finally, after lying in bed for several minutes, he pulled himself up. He put on his shoes and gave a passing glance at himself in the mirror, doing his best to straighten out his hair. His reflection looked like he'd seen better days, but that didn't come as much of a surprise. These past few months on the road had been hard at times, and the next journey in front of him didn't sound like it was going to be that easy. Still he wouldn't be alone this time. They might not make the best of companions, Ishandra and especially Mark, but having people around might not be so bad.

Mark and Ishandra were sitting at the table when he exited the bedroom. They both turned to look at him, gauging his condition. Ishandra broke the silence between them. "Thomas, how are you feeling?" she asked, her voice showing her softer side once again.

"Better, I think. The nap helped."

"That's good, I know it was a lot to take in at once." He gave her a nod at that.

"So," Mark began, speaking with a slight hesitation, "will you come with us?"

Will A. Sanborn

Thomas paused as it was his turn to study the two of them. He focused his attention on Mark and asked "and if I didn't want to go along...?"

Mark shook his head and the fire in his eyes dimmed. "If you're thinking we're going to kidnap you son, you don't need to worry about that. We think you should come along with us, but we're not going to force you."

"So I could walk away just like that?"

Mark just gave him a small nod. He glanced over at Ishandra, she had her eyes cast down slightly and looked resigned to letting him leave. Thomas paused for effect, and then continued "okay, I'm in then." He gave them both a smile, and it felt very genuine as he saw their reactions.

Mark's eyes lit up and the man gave him a sly grin of his own; his lips parted wider as he nodded his head. "Very good" he said as he let out a small chuckle. Then he took Thomas' hand in his firm grasp again. "Thank you for trusting us, Thomas."

"You're welcome," Thomas replied, but his voice was lower. Now that he was committed, he hoped he'd made the right decision.

"Ishandra is happy to have you come along too," Mark said, giving Thomas a sly wink and squeezing his hand as he shook it.

Thomas shot another glance at Ishandra and she was smiling at him as well; her eyes were bright. She gave a little nod in reply to Mark and Thomas felt his face heating up again.

◆ ◆ ◆

Ishandra and Mark made quick work of packing their clothes and supplies, and within ten minutes they were ready to go. Each of them carried a large duffle bag, packed full with their essentials. Thomas had only the clothes he'd been wearing the night before, and his wallet, so he offered to carry Ishandra's bag. She declined his offer, but said he was sweet to ask, and then gave him a quick peck on the cheek for doing so. Mark watched on and appeared not to feel much one way or another about that; his attention seemed focused more on them getting moving.

They locked up the trailer, and then went to settle affairs with management at main tent. Thomas watched Ishandra as she talked with the man for a few minutes. From what he could gather, it sounded as if she had very little dependence on the people running the carnival and they let her have whatever freedom she wanted. The man said that they could get by without her for awhile and that they'd look after the trailer for her and Mark. He wished her well on her vacation and that was that.

They passed several people on their way out who wanted to know where they were going. Mark and Ishandra gave a vague excuse of needing to get away from it all. A few people were curious about whom Thomas was, but they were content to just be introduced to him. One woman though, a tall amazon bodybuilder, asked Ishandra who her new boyfriend was. She seemed amused at making Thomas blush, but gave him a friendly slap on the shoulder as they were leaving. "Bye cutie, hope to see you around sometime..."

"Thomas, what are you driving for vehicle?" Mark asked him as they exited the gates of the carnival and walked out into the parking area.

"Uh, a Subaru."

"Do you mind if we take it? A sedan would be more comfortable than my truck."

Thomas paused. "I guess so."

"That way if you decide to leave, you'll have your own vehicle," Ishandra offered. He nodded, that idea did have its merits.

"Okay, but I just realized. I don't have that much money left for driving around. It's been a week since I last worked and I was going to have to look for an odd job or so pretty soon to get some more cash."

Ishandra simply smiled and reached into one of her pockets to retrieve a small wallet. She opened it and pulled out a wad of bills. She handed two of them to Thomas and he gasped as he saw they were one-hundred dollar notes. "Ishandra..."

"I've had enough time to accumulate some wealth, hon" she said. "It's more than enough to live on and certainly enough to take care of our expenses on this journey." He stared at the money and she curled his fingers around it with her hand, forcing it into his fist. He thanked her, and as they headed off to his car, he slipped the cash into his wallet.

◆ ◆ ◆

By the time they'd loaded up his car and got on the road, it was already the afternoon. They wasted no time in getting going though, and as soon as they could get to it they were on the highway headed east. Ishandra sat in the front passenger seat, while Mark sat behind her. They talked a little bit from time to time, but mostly spent the trip in silence. Thomas didn't mind the quiet, as it gave him more time to think. He wondered where they were going. There was a large chunk of the country ahead of them as they headed away from the West Coast. Would they be able to find their intended destination by chance, or would providence show them the way?

They'd been driving for several hours when they made a stop to gas up. Ishandra went inside the small convenience store, leaving Thomas alone with Mark. The older man got out to stand beside him as Thomas pumped gas.

"How are you doing?" he asked in reply to Thomas' glance in his direction.

"Okay, I guess... It's still a lot to figure out, all this stuff about magic and religion."

Mark nodded. "It can be a lot to take in, that's for sure. Give it a little time." He paused, and then added "how about Ishandra and I, are you okay with that?"

Will A. Sanborn

"Um, I guess so. I mean if you're okay with it..." Thomas stared back at Mark. He searched his face for signs of his intentions, but the man's expression stayed stoic.

"We've been together a long time, son. We've made the agreements and set boundaries. I'm used to this, and I am okay with it. What I want to make sure is that you'll be alright with how things are."

Thomas didn't say anything, so Mark continued. "Ishandra likes you, and that's fine, but we'll be sharing her attentions. It doesn't bother me, but I want to make sure it sits well with you." He paused then finished with "besides, I don't want you looking over your shoulder at me every time the two of you share a moment."

"I'm sorry, I didn't know how to act" Thomas heard himself say as he dropped his eyes from Mark's gaze.

"You don't need to apologize, that's what I'm trying to tell you. Ishandra and I care about each other, but I don't own her."

Thomas waited through an eternal debate, and then finally asked. "Do you mind if I ask you why, Mark?"

"Why what?"

"Why are things like that?" He had more pointed questions, but he didn't voice them.

"That's how she is, son. I've been around long enough to realize that you take love where you can find it. If you find someone you fit with, you stick with them."

"It really doesn't bother you?"

"I'm too old to get jealous. Besides, at my age, I'm not always in the mood, so I let her find companionship when she wants to. I know she's coming back to me. Plus, she's a good judge of character." He grinned and clapped Thomas on the shoulder. Thomas returned his smile a moment later, when he realized Mark's compliment.

"You're a good kid, Thomas" Mark added. "You're a little unsure of things, but more time spent living will take care of that. I'm happy to have you along with us."

"Thanks Mark" Thomas replied, as his smile grew wider and he felt really at ease for the first time that day.

◆ ◆ ◆

Because they'd gotten off to a late start, they'd driven on into the night, trying to make as much progress as possible. Mark took over driving after awhile. Thomas was tired enough that he didn't turn down the offer. When they finally stopped for the night, they were all ready to turn in. Besides Ishandra's bed the night before, Thomas had been sleeping a good deal in the back of his car, to stretch his money a little further. A hotel bed was sounding pretty good to him just then. They'd gotten two rooms, and when Ishandra handed him a key, he didn't question the situation. He said good night to them and brought his own duffle bag into his empty room.

He was getting ready for bed when he heard the knock on his door. He quickly finished brushing his teeth and rinsed his mouth out with a swig of water. He then answered the door to find Ishandra there. He wasn't surprised that it was her, though he was a little surprised that she'd dropped in on him at all.

"Mark wants to spend the night together" she said as she entered his room.

"I figured as much."

"I know, hon, but I wanted to make sure you know that I care about you."

"Okay" he said, not really sure how to reply.

"I mean it, Thomas" she said as she moved to sit down on the edge of the bed and motioned for him to join her.

He sat down facing her. "I was serious when I said everything about you this morning. I do think you're special, and I want to spend more time with you. Mark and I will work things out so I have time for you as well."

He nodded, but stayed silent. He felt awkward in front of her again, despite having enthusiastically shared a bed with her the night before.

She stared at him with those deep green eyes, as if trying to read him once again. "You look cute in your nightclothes" she said as she gestured to the pair of shorts and the comfortable faded old t-shirt he wore.

He smiled at her and without even thinking of it, leaned in to plant a gentle kiss on the tip of her snout. The tension between them melted away and she responded and kissed him back. He felt her mouth open against his as their lips met. With his eyes closed he pulled her against him, his arms wrapping around her back.

She reciprocated and he felt her arms holding him. Her fingers stroked him in slow movements as he clutched at her back. He felt her thin tongue pushing against his as their kiss deepened. He let out a low, guttural moan as he pressed his body against her and felt her respond.

She let out her own growl of arousal, but then he felt her slowing down. She eased up on her kisses; she moved so as not to be abrupt, but eventually pulled away from his lips. He looked at her as she moved her head back, and met her sheepish expression.

"I'm sorry, Thomas. I promised Mark I'd spend tonight with him, and we keep our promises to each other." She paused, letting out a rueful little laugh. "I didn't mean to get you all worked up just to leave you alone. You don't deserve that. I promise I'll make it up to you tomorrow."

She reached out to touch the side of his face, and as she did so he gave her fingers a gentle kiss. His eyes were starting to water, but he gave her a nod of understanding. Her own eyes were brimming and she smiled at his gesture.

"Come on, hon, let's get you to bed" she said as she took his hand. She rose up and led him to the head of the bed. Then she turned down the sheets and helped him into it, and finally pulled the covers over him. "You've been

Will A. Sanborn

through a lot today and have risen to the challenges quite bravely. Get some sleep and tomorrow will be a little easier."

He felt his eyes starting to burn with his tears as he stared up at her, but he didn't care. He reached his hands up and pulled her down into a hug. They stayed like that for several minutes as he drank in her warmth. Finally, when she did have to ease away and leave him, he whispered "thank you" to her as she was turning off the light next to his bed. She smiled and silently left his room. She left him alone, but he was still surrounded by her warmth as he closed his eyes. He lay there and hugged himself, remembering her presence. He fell into sleep shortly afterwards, worn out by the events of the day. His dreams might have been troubled, but if they were he didn't remember any of them.

Will A. Sanborn

Chapter 6: Breakfast of the Gods

Hello, how are you? I know you, I knew you
I think I can remember your name
Hello, I'm sorry I lost myself
I think I thought you were someone else
Should we talk about the weather?
Should we talk about the government?
* R.E.M., "Pop Song 89"*

If God had a face, what would it look like?
And would you want to see?
If seeing meant that you would have to believe
In things like Heaven and in Jesus and the Saints
And all the Prophets
* Joan Osborne, "One of Us"*

"Ugh, I definitely don't like long bus rides!" Anubis exclaimed as they moved away from the crowd that was exiting the Greyhound bus.

"I thought you liked being around the living so much," Thoth said as he cocked his head and gave the tired jackal a wink.

"Yes, I still like humanity, but not in such close quarters. I'd rather be in a bigger city where there are more exotics to blend in with too. Those kids who kept asking us questions were getting tiring."

"Well, you did want some attention."

"Very funny, hon. Now I just want a break from it. I can't wait until we get into the next city and can stop for a shower."

"That won't be until late tonight, I think" Thoth replied, then added "at least we can get something to eat. Maybe breakfast will cheer you up."

◆ ◆ ◆

Thomas, Mark and Ishandra had stopped for breakfast at a restaurant at one of the rest-areas along the highway. It wasn't the greatest food, but the greasy-spoon was a step above McDonald's and even Denny's. Thomas was sure used to worse from his weeks on the road. It felt nice to have an occasional sit-down meal, even if it wasn't the classiest of joints and they made omelets and pancakes as well as the next place.

They'd all gotten their food and had started eating when they were approached by a couple of strangers. Thomas looked up and was surprised to see two exotics walking towards their table. One of them appeared to be a canine of some sort, with dark black fur and the other was some kind of avian, another rare type of exotic.

"Hello, I hope you'll pardon the intrusion during your meal," the bird-man said, "but I think you might be someone we'd like to talk to."

Mark appeared nonplussed, but Thomas saw a gleam of interest in Ishandra's eyes. "Yes, please join us" she said as she motioned for the two of them to sit down.

The avian took the empty seat at the booth next to Thomas and his canine friend grabbed a chair from a nearby table and brought it over. After sitting down, the avian offered his hand to Ishandra. "Thank you for your hospitality."

The dragoness took his hand, and held onto it for a few seconds. The gleam in her eyes grew stronger and a smile appeared on her muzzle. She gave a knowing nod to the ibis and simply said "I think introductions are in order, I'm Ishandra, this is my husband mark, and our friend Thomas." She paused, then added "I gather you can sense that there's something different about me... as I can you."

Thoth returned her nod. "Yes Ishandra, when we first saw you, I thought you might be another of the older goddesses, but I wasn't sure until we sat down. It is nice meeting another member of one of the old dynasties out here, and certainly unexpected. Oh forgive me, I am Thoth, and this is Anubis. We're from the Egyptian realm."

Thomas was staring at the newcomers, his mind a buzz with new questions. He didn't get a chance to voice them right just then, for the waitress had returned to check up on them. She was surprised to see two more exotic diners at the table, but she regained her composure quickly and took their orders like a true professional. Thoth ordered the steak and eggs and Anubis ordered a Belgian waffle with strawberries and whipped cream.

When the waitress departed, they were free to continue their discussion. "So what brings the two of you all the way out here?" Ishandra asked. "I imagine you're doing more than just sight-seeing. I haven't met anybody from your continent in ages, and the last one was one of the Greeks."

Thoth gave her a wink in response to both her question and the knowing look she'd given him. "I imagine you've detected an unbalance in the force of magic somewhere in this country?"

"Sort of, I'm not as sensitive to magic as I used to be. It was Mark who found out about it." Thoth cocked his head at her and she answered his unspoken question. "He was contacted by an angel of Jehovah's associate, the god without a name. It was her who warned him that something was posing a threat to this world."

"Hmmm, very curious indeed... I didn't think the new gods had much contact with the living anymore" Thoth pondered aloud. "I guess on occasion it still must be necessary. It also confirms my worry that whatever it is behind the mysterious force is likely to be dangerous."

Thoth paused, then motioned towards Thomas, "and he, has he been in contact with any of the gods as well?"

Will A. Sanborn

"No, only me," Ishandra said with a slight chuckle. "He's just a mortal, though the angel hinted that there'd be someone who'd be important on our quest, and we both think it might be him."

Thomas didn't know how to feel about being referred to indirectly in that manner. He forced a slight smile for Ishandra though. He then noticed that Anubis was smirking at him. The jackal caused one of his ears to flick when he caught the human looking at him.

"Very interesting," Thoth remarked. "I've never seen the gods of different dynasties work together like this before."

Ishandra nodded. "So do you have any more idea what this disturbance you're detecting is?"

"No, I only came out to investigate more out of curiosity. You know that we no longer have a stake in this world, but we both are still interested in what the living are doing these days, Anubis especially." The jackal lowered his ears slightly at that remark and gave Thoth a playful swat on the hand.

"Well, your affinity to magic sounds like it could be quite useful, especially given how you can detect it from so far away. Would you be interested in traveling with us?" She turned to her companions and then asked "Mark and Thomas, is that okay with you guys?"

Mark nodded, "sure, I think any help we can get on this would be good. Glad to have you guys aboard."

Thomas felt their eyes upon him. He wasn't sure what to say. He felt a little uneasy about having to make the decision about these two new strangers, and more gods no less, but he also didn't want to be holding up the party. Again he felt like a pawn in the moves which were unfolding before him. "Um, yeah, that'd be okay. It's really up to you guys anyway, since you've got more experience in dealing with this sort of thing."

"But it's your car," Ishandra added.

"You have a car?" Anubis asked; his ears perked up as he spoke. "Oh, it'd be so nice to get out of that damn bus."

Thomas had to smile in spite of himself. "Well, it's going to be a bit tight with all five of us, but I've fit that many in there for trips before." He paused, smiling at the jackal's enthusiasm, and then added "sure, you guys are welcome to come along with us."

"Thank you" Anubis said as he eagerly reached out his hand to shake it with Thomas'.

"You're welcome, though I can't begin to say how surreal this is getting for me. I thought it was weird enough with one ancient goddess, but now you guys show up... I took a mythology class in school. You were the god of the dead, weren't you? I'd never believed those stories could possibly be true..."

He stopped as he saw Anubis' expression darken and the jackal's ears drooped once again. Anubis stared at him for several moments, without saying a word. He then muttered that he needed to be excused and stood up to walk away from the table. They watched him go as he headed back towards the pay phones and rest rooms.

Thomas felt a knot tighten in his stomach. He turned to look at Thoth, who was looking at him with those bird-like eyes. "What did I do?" Thomas heard himself ask, his voice was hushed.

"I'm sorry, but my companion is very sensitive to our roll in the scheme of things now. He's never gotten over our dynasty falling. You're probably the first human in a long time who has known his true identity, and it was a bit embarrassing for him."

"I'm sorry, I didn't know..." Thomas' words trailed off again. Ishandra reached out her hand to touch his and gave him a reassuring look.

"It's okay," Thoth replied. "He can be very moody at times. He's just a little upset and he'll get over it. To tell you the truth, I think this trip is good for him, it gives him something to think about and keeps him distracted. I think he likes you, so he'll soon forget it."

Thoth waited a few minutes, and then excused himself to go and check on his companion. They both returned a couple of minutes later. Anubis was quieter than he had been. Thomas tried to spend the rest of the meal avoiding the jackal's gaze. It was lucky that the waitress brought the two newcomer's meals soon afterwards, so they all had something to focus their attention on.

When he was done eating, Thomas felt awkward again as they waited for the two Egyptians to finish their food. Finally they all were finished and it was time to pay the bill and get back on the road again. It was going to be tight enough in the car as it was, and it would be even more uncomfortable with the unfinished business between him and Anubis. He hesitated as they were walking out. The jackal headed to the rest room again, presumably to wash the gooey remnants of the Belgian waffle out of the fur on of his face. Thomas handed his keys to Mark and told him he'd catch up to them in a bit. Mark nodded and headed out with Ishandra and Thoth. Thomas caught a gleam in the dragoness' eye and an encouraging smile on her face, as she gave him a quick look over her shoulder.

Thomas waited in the hallway for a couple of minutes, feeling his stomach begin to churn all over again. Finally Anubis emerged and gave him a surprised look as he saw the human waiting for him.

"Uh, I wanted to apologize for before" Thomas said. "In talking to Ishandra, I know she's lost a lot, and I should've realized that you have too. It's got to be hard for you to be left behind like this... I'm just not used to dealing with this. Heck, a day ago I never even knew this was possible."

Anubis' expression brightened and his ears perked up. "And I should apologize too, Thomas. It's been quite some time since I've really interacted with a mortal, and I've forgotten how different your world is now."

"So things are okay?" Thomas asked after a couple of seconds' hesitation. It was the best thing he could think of saying.

Anubis nodded, "yes, I think they are, and it's very sweet of you to make amends like this."

Thomas offered Anubis his hand and saw that the jackal's tail was twitching slightly behind him. Anubis took his hand, but instead of just shaking it, he pulled Thomas into a hug, wrapping his arms around him. Thomas let out a gasp of surprise, but then relaxed against Anubis. He even managed to put one arm loosely around the jackal, returning the gesture. It felt awkward, but at least he no longer had the dull ache of worry eating away at the pit of his stomach.

He held the embrace for what seemed to be an appropriate amount of time, and then gently pulled away. As he disentangled himself from the jackal's arms, Anubis smiled at him. "Thank you, Thomas."

"Sure, no problem. I'm just glad things are okay." Thomas still felt a little odd around Anubis, but it felt good to have cleared the air between them.

♦ ♦ ♦

The driving was pretty much uneventful that morning. Ishandra had taken the front passenger seat and since Mark had decided to do the driving to start off with, that meant Thomas was sitting in back with Anubis and Thoth. Things went fine though. They managed to get a conversation going, and after awhile, Anubis even brought up some information about the old times in ancient Egypt. When he was talking, it was quite easy to see so how proud he was. While he was telling Thomas all about it, his spirits seemed to be lifted as well. Thomas found everything fascinating, but kept on having to remind himself that it was actually happening, and he was indeed riding in a car with three ancient deities.

They hit the Rocky Mountains in the afternoon and were driving over the continental divide a few hours later. They made a stop at Independence Pass. They might be on some sort of a holy quest, but they still weren't going to miss out on an opportunity to do a little sight-seeing, especially one such as good as that.

Thomas got out of the car and wandered a bit away from the group. He felt the need to get away for a little bit, to think things over, and looking at the mountains gave him a good chance to do that. It was a beautiful day and the mountain air felt wonderful as he took in a deep breath. The sky was clear and blue and the sun shone off the mountains; a recent early-autumn storm had left the peaks covered in snow. It was a reminder of the colder weather coming in the months to follow, while the air was warm enough to enjoy the spectacle without the need for jackets. Even with everything that could concern his mind, it was hard to get too upset looking at the view, at least for awhile anyway.

He happened to glance back at the others and he noticed that Anubis had his arm around Thoth. He looked a little closer and saw that the jackal had his hand resting on the ibis' back. The way he was touching him as they stood together suggested that they were a bit more than just travel companions. That explained things a little bit, as he remembered the way Anubis had hugged him. As he watched the two of them and thought about it though, it didn't really bother him. It was odd and different, but he couldn't really find it disturbing.

With everything he'd seen recently, finding out the two male Egyptian gods were probably lovers as well as friends didn't seem to matter that much. He found himself smiling a little bit over that thought as he turned his attention back to the mountains. 'Strange days indeed.'

He was so lost in his thoughts and the wonderful view, that he was a little surprised when he heard Mark come up behind him.

"Beautiful day for it?" Mark asked after Thomas turned around to see him.

"Yes, it's amazing."

"That it is. Whenever I see something like this, I can't help but think about the glory of God to have created this splendor."

Thomas mulled that over that for a couple of moments before asking "but what about God, Mark? We've got two examples of other, older gods now. If they exist, does that mean there's multiple gods, and if so, how do you know who created the world? How do you know who to follow?"

"I used to ponder that question after I'd met Ishandra, son. I thought about it enough to make my mind go around in circles, so I gave it up." Mark paused to look Thomas directly in the eyes. "All I know is that the God I follow has showed His hand in my life before. I can't profess to understand it all, but maybe it doesn't matter. There was a higher power that helped create this world, and there are powers we cannot see going on behind the scenes." He finally finished with "I know my God is real, and that's good enough for me."

There wasn't much Thomas could do say to that. He simply nodded and turned his eyes back to the majesty of nature that was before him. He'd never had much faith in his adult life; it'd fallen away gradually since childhood. Now that there seemed to be mounting proof to God's existence, the thought of it unnerved him. If he had proof, did that mean that faith was irrelevant? Did he have no choice but to believe?

They stood there for many minutes; the silence between them went unheeded as they gazed out at the mountains. Thomas felt the view southing to his troubled mind, and before he even realized he was doing it, he closed his eyes and thought of his thankfulness for the moment of peace. It was less a prayer than it was a meditation, for it was directed at nobody in particular. It still helped though.

Afterwards the two of them made their way back to the car. "Aren't the mountains wonderful?" Ishandra asked them as they returned to join the rest of the group. "No matter how many times I see them, I'm still struck by their beauty."

Thomas nodded, and then turned to the Egyptians. "What about you guys, what do you think?"

"They're quite nice" Thoth remarked, they remind me of the ones out in Europe." Thomas had to chuckle at his reaction to hearing that; of course they'd all seen more then him. Even Mark, who was only human, probably still had a good twenty-five years of experience on him.

"What's so amusing?" Anubis asked.

"Oh, I just realized how naive I must appear to you guys. You've all seen and done so much, compared to me.

"There's nothing wrong with that, it's nice to be able to look at the world with new eyes. Enjoy it while you can and maybe you can help us to do the same."

Anubis sounded sincere in his words and they didn't come across as bitter or moody. Thomas smiled at that.

◆ ◆ ◆

When they reached the hotel that evening, Thomas went inside with Ishandra and Mark as they got the room keys. He looked around at the front desk and soon found what he wanted. Off to the side there was a small stand of post cards. He picked out one with a good picture of the Rockies on it and gave the desk clerk the fifty cents to purchase it.

"A souvenir of the trip?" Ishandra asked him.

"Not exactly, I should be sending one home."

"Oh...?" Ishandra mused.

Thomas knew she wasn't going to let him off without an explanation, so he elaborated. "It's for my folks. I don't get to call them much. We don't do that well talking that is, so I send them a post card or a letter when I get the chance, just to let them know I'm okay."

Ishandra nodded. "It won't always have to be that way, hon. With a little more time passing and you thinking things over some more, you might be able to work through things with them.

Thomas managed to give her a solemn nod. "So, are you going to tell them all about us?" she asked as she flashed him a warm smile.

"Heh, no I don't think they're ready for all of that," he said, as he felt her humor and warmth infecting his mood.

46   Will A. Sanborn

Chapter 7: Take Some Time with a Friend, Take Some Time for Love

Even on the night when empty promise means empty hand
And soldiers coming home like shadows turning red
When the lights of hope are fading quickly then look to me
I'll be your homing angel, I'll be in your head
Because you're lonely in your nightmare let me in
And there's heat beneath your winter let me in
*   Duran Duran, "Lonely in Your Nightmare"*

You make me lose my body
And nothing could be better
You make me lose my body
It's like we've died and gone to heaven
*   Devo, "When We Do It"*

"Today was another interesting day," Ishandra said as they sat on the bed in their hotel room. Thomas nodded in agreement; it certainly had been another strange day. "I'm proud of you for how you're holding up through all of this" she continued.

He simply shrugged at that, "I'm just trying to get through it."

"No, Thomas, you're doing more than that" she replied as she rested her hand on his arm. Her touch felt warm and comforting. "You're really rising to the occasion here, like how you patched things up with Anubis this morning." She paused, and then added "what do you think of our new friends?"

"They're okay. Anubis seems like he's a little dramatic, but he rubs off on you. I think he's someone I'm going to really like though."

Ishandra smiled. "Yes, he does seem like the emotional type, but like you said I think he could end up being a good person to know. His enthusiasm is infectious when he's in a happy mood. They make a cute couple too, or hadn't you noticed?"

Thomas nodded, "yeah, I'd noticed."

"Thoth's quiet reserved attitude balances out Anubis' emotional side well." She paused again, then added "Anubis likes you, Thomas." Thomas stared back at her and watched wordlessly as her smile grew. "You did see him warming up to you didn't you?"

"Well yes..."

"I think he found you just attractive at first, which might have been why he overacted to your comments at breakfast this morning. But listening to the two of you talking this afternoon as he told you more about Egypt, it was obvious he was appreciating you as a person. You've won him over in more ways than one..."

Thomas felt the familiar sensation of his face becoming flushed. "I hadn't realized that" he said as he averted her gaze.

"Relax hon, it doesn't mean anything bad, you should be flattered. I think it's sweet and it shows that you are something special... Is it so bad that another male finds you attractive? It doesn't mean that you have to do anything."

"I've just never thought about it before. It's just odd..."

"It'll be okay hon. He doesn't seem like the type of person to force himself on anyone, so you can just ignore or appreciate his affections for what they are." She reached out to touch his cheek, "I think you're really cute when you blush like that."

"Oh really?" he said, as he stuck out his lower lip and pretended to pout.

She chuckled at that. "You're really special to me, Thomas."

His expression grew more serious. He stared back at her, and looked at the face of the beautiful dragoness who was gazing upon him with those expressive green eyes of hers. "You are too, Ishandra. Spending time with you means a lot to me." He hesitated, trying to pull the words together. "I like you, but I still don't know how to feel about all of this..."

"It still feels like it's happening too quickly, hon?"

He nodded. It wasn't all that surprising that she knew what he was trying to say, but it felt like she wanted him to continue. "I can't say I love you yet, Ishandra, but I care for you and want to be with you."

"Love takes time. We can give each other comfort and friendship now though. There's nothing wrong or mystical about that, and I want to share that with you, Thomas. I know that you wouldn't be doing anything if you didn't feel some connection between us."

He nodded again. "I do feel it."

"It's genuine hon, and it's more than just attraction, you can trust in that." She then added, "and you don't need to worry about any spells from me giving you a push this time." She gave him another smile for reassurance, but she still felt the ripple of uncertainty pass within him.

"It still seems weird to be with an ancient goddess."

"It's not all that different hon. It's not like I shoot lightning bolts out of my fingers or anything. We're both just flesh and blood."

"I've never been with an older woman before..." Thomas added and gave her a playful smile. His smile grew wider as he heard her respond with warm laughter.

"You have such a wonderful spirit. I really hope I can spend the time with you to see you grow into all of your potential."

He leaned forward and threw his arms around her. She responded, pulling him towards her and he melted into her warm embrace. "Thank you," he whispered as he leaned his head on her shoulder.

He sighed as he felt the comforting warmth of her body next to his. He heard her breath escape her mouth in agreement as he held her close. It was an affirmation without words; no words were needed as they basked in the warmth

Will A. Sanborn

of each other's presence. He closed his eyes and nuzzled her neck with a gentle motion. She sighed again as he did so.

He held her against him, and his hands moved along her back; they traced the contours of her body with idle movements. He was lost in the moment and he let his hands wander over her in slow, fluid motions. She responded and he felt her give him a gentle squeeze as she pushed his body against hers. He let his breath escape again as they stroked each other softly. It felt safe and warm, loving and giving, gentle yet hinting at a smoldering eagerness. It felt like being home, and like being in love.

The minutes ticked out as they continued their gentle caresses, content at the moment with sharing the simple pleasures that the warmth of closeness and simple touches could bring. He gave her another whimper as he pressed himself against her. He grasped at her briefly, pulling her towards him as he tightened their embrace and accented the closeness between them. Then he eased up and returned to his gentle caresses.

He felt her respond in kind. He also felt her breath hot on the side of his face and down on his neck. A moment later he felt the soft touch of her tongue on the tip of his ear. It tickled at first and a little shiver ran through him as her supple tongue deftly licked at his flesh. She released a soft moan from him as he drank in her attentions, and he gave her body another squeeze.

He moved his head to look up at her and saw those green eyes looking back at him. Her eyes were bright with emotion as she regarded him. Her mouth was open slightly, her lips parted and he saw her tongue dart out in a quick motion as it played up across her snout.

He leaned in and his lips met hers. Their first kiss was gentle, a prelude and a promise of more to come. He closed his eyes and stroked his hands in a slow movement up her back. He could feel the warmth between them growing slowly, but building steadily. She pulled him closer and her mouth opened against his. He felt their kiss deepen and heard the low sighs they both made.

He responded and parted his lips wider to meet hers. He pressed his mouth against hers and reveled in the tingles of excitement which started to stir within him. His hands clutched at her as they kissed. He pulled her to him as his tongue slipped into her mouth, tentative at first, then more daring. He felt her own lithe tongue brushing against his and he heard another low moan emanate from the back of her throat.

He gave out a whimper as well, as he relished in the fullness of their embrace. He could feel the heat of her body against his, even through their clothes, and the growing arousal between them as they continued to kiss. He tasted her as she sampled him, and he savored the warm wetness of their mouths joining. He felt the gentle, but growing, insistency of their tongues intertwining.

The moments were lost between them as they continued to embrace; they groped one another as they kissed deeply and surrendered themselves to the passion between them. He let out another moan and then eased off on the kiss.

He slid his lips from her with a slow deliberateness; he drew out their contact while still pulling away. When he'd broken contact he opened his eyes to look at her again, to see her smiling face looking back at him. The heat between them was reflected in her eyes.

He hugged her again and stuck his tongue out to lick at her snout playfully. His arms slowly found their way to her sides, and then up along her clothing. She was dressed in gypsy's garb, complete with a tan bodice over a simple white shirt. His hands came to rest at the laces of the bodice and he smiled at her as his fingers toyed with the knot.

She returned his smile. Her green eyes shone brightly as she looked up at him and waited for his move. Her tongue darted out once more as he gave a gentle tug at the knot. He pulled on it with a slow, deliberate motion, as he slipped the bonds apart. The knot loosened and the two laces came undone. His hands moved faster then. He could feel his smile spreading wider on his lips as he pulled at the bodice. The two halves of the garment parted as the bodice opened up, revealing the buttons of her shirt below them.

He pushed the tan fabric aside and turned his attention to the shirt which still covered her. He popped the first button loose, and then slipped his fingers in to touch the nape of her neck. He heard her exhale a deep breath as he stroked her there. Then, moving just as deliberately as before, he brought his fingers downward, to tackle each button in turn. Her shirt opened slightly as he undid the buttons one after another and his fingers slid down over her skin. He found the indentation of her navel and stroked his touch along its contours. She gave him another sigh in return for his attentions.

With the last of the buttons taken care of, he gently parted the opening of her shirt, to reveal her hidden beauty beneath it. He slid the garment up and back, his fingers tracing over her smooth blue skin as he did so. He slipped the shirt over her shoulders, then down and off of her. She was stripped to waist, and open to his approving gaze. Those beautiful eyes of hers watched him as he looked upon her.

"You're so beautiful" he whispered to her as he reached out a hand to gently cup one of her breasts. His fingers slid across her nipple, to touch her sensitive flesh as he examined the darker-blue skin there. She sighed at his touch. He brought his lips against hers and their mouths joined in another kiss.

Her tongue found his again as he held her. His hand found his way down her back, sliding along her spine until it came to rest against the top of her tail. He felt the kiss deepen once again and he cupped her breast with his hand. He squeezed it as he pulled her against him once more. His hand slid down to make a gentle grope of her butt through her skirt, as his fingers bunched up the fabric.

She was the one to make the next move. She slowly eased her mouth away from his, and pulled her head back away from him in a gentle motion. Her eyes watched him as she took his hand in hers and extracted herself from his

50   Will A. Sanborn

caressing touch. She held onto his hand for the moment, and traced her fingers along his palm. She was smiling as she got up to stand before him.

She watched him silently, without uttering a word as her hands slowly traced down the side of her body. They came to rest at the hem of her skirt. The blue skin of her body was in sharp contract to the reddish-brown earth tone of the fabric. Her fingers slid along the edge of it, their slow motions teased him as she stared into his eyes. Her smile grew wider as she saw his eyes following the contours of her body, and she watched him watching her.

She undid the button of the skirt, and then turned slowly away from him with fluid grace. She turned away so he could see her side and then her back. Her hands reached back and released the clasp above her tail with a gentle deftness. The loop of fabric gave way and slipped down, revealing the part in the skirt which her tail passed through. With nothing holding it to her, the garment started to slide. The beautiful dragoness gave no resistance and let gravity take the skirt from her. It slid down, over her butt and then down her legs, to land in a rumpled pile on the floor.

Ishandra looked back over her shoulder at Thomas. Her expression showed her approval at his appreciation of her nearly-naked body. His eyes took in the full sight of her; he drank in the cobalt hue of her skin and all of her exotic beauty. His gaze wandered down her back to take in the sight of her lovely butt and tail. When she was satisfied with the view she'd given him, she slowly turned once again to face him. It was then that Thomas caught sight of her panties.

Her underwear was cut slightly different than normal. Like the rest of her clothing, it'd been modified to work with her exotic body. He underwear sat along her front like it normally would, but it didn't cover all of her butt. It rode lower, coming to rest at the base of her tail, covering her delicate areas, but not giving discomfort. It wasn't until she'd turned around that Thomas could get a good look at what she was wearing, and when he did finally see it, he was in for an amusing surprise.

Ishandra was wearing a delicate set of pink panties, the fabric of which was adorned with many small little hearts. The darker-pink valentine shapes covered the entire garment and gave it a slightly girly look. It was definitely feminine and adorably cute, but it wasn't something he'd expected Ishandra to be wearing. The surprise of it brought another smile to his face.

"I see you approve of these," Ishandra said with a chuckle in her voice as her hands came to rest beside her panties. She swayed her hips just slightly from side to side as she spoke.

Thomas nodded and laughed with her. "They're a little out of character, but very cute."

"I thought you'd enjoy them, hon. I get in mood to indulge in silly, soft things once in awhile." She paused, and then added "they're pretty, aren't they?" as her fingers slipped into the waistband on one side.

He nodded again. The soft pink of her panties was a lovely contract against the deep blue of her skin. She took a step closer to him, coming within his reach. He reached up to trace his fingers up her legs, and came to rest his touch along the edge of her undies. He felt the softness of the fabric against her smooth skin. He slid his fingers sideways, gliding his fingers over the thin bit of cloth separating her from his touch. She sighed softly as his fingers hovered over the center of her crotch.

He glanced up and met her gaze for a moment, then returned his attention to her panties. He reached up to grasp the waistband and his fingers slid against hers as he did so. Then he began to pull down, peeling the delicate bit of fabric away from her. His hands trailed along the sides of her buttocks as he edged her panties down, revealing her bit by bit to his eyes. A moment later the slit of her vulva was exposed as he pulled the pink bit of cotton away from her blue skin. He'd seen her body before, the first night they'd been together, but he still couldn't help and let a gasp escape his mouth as he saw her exposed to him. He heard the dragoness let out a happy sigh in response.

He moved quicker once her secrets were uncovered. With a long fluid motion he slid the panties down her leg. When he reached her feet, she stepped out of them with delicate grace. He let the soft garment fall from his grasp and straightened up to regard her once again. She moved her feet apart, opening herself to him. He'd brought his hand to rest against the edge of her crotch and hesitated there.

Her hand found his and gave it a gentle nudge, guiding it closer. That was all the encouragement he needed. He traced his fingers along the opening of her sex, and then slowly slid inside. He heard the hiss of her breath as he slipped his touch inside her. His fingers probed her gently, feeling her warm wetness.

Her hand covered his and urged him onward; her touch pressed their fingers deeper inside her. She let out a moan and she moved forward, and arched her back as she pressed herself against his touch. Thomas was suddenly distinctly aware of his own arousal. He felt the ache growing in his groin and he tightened his pelvic muscles. His cock twitched and sent a shiver through him as he and Ishandra's fingers continued to play with her pussy.

She leaned forward and put her other hand on his shoulder. She pressed her belly against the side of his face and reached up to stroke his head. He felt her skin against his cheek. He nuzzled her with his head as their intertwined hands were still busy inside her. He flexed his fingers against her and felt her body react.

He continued his ministrations with her aid. Their touch invaded her, and she opened up further to the probing of their fingers. She moved her legs; her thighs came together slightly and then he could feel her tighten against their fingers. Her body held him in a warm grasp and he pushed against the slick contours of her cunny. The whimper of pleasure that fell from her lips spurred him on. At the same time his other hand had found his own crotch and he idly

Will A. Sanborn

started stroking his erection through his pants. His sigh mingled with hers as he felt the sparks of pleasure shoot through him.

Moments passed and then her hand tightened on his; her grasp slowed his attentions. He followed her cue and slowly withdrew from her. He elicited another gasp of her breath as he did so. His fingers were covered with her arousal and he delicately wiped the wetness covering them over her inner thigh as his fingers slid away from her sex. As he looked up at her, her hand came down to join his at his crotch and he felt the quick squeeze of her grasp. He stiffed against her touch and held his breath.

She held him like that for a few moments and then released him. "I think it's time we got you out of these clothes, hon" she said as her hands tugged on his shirt.

He offered no resistance and became submissive to her touch. He lifted his hands so she could pull the shirt off of him. The feel of the fabric sliding against his skin tickled his nerves. She tossed his shirt on the floor and her fingers slid along his chest and tummy. Her touch rewarded him for his loving care towards her earlier, and she was eager to return the favor. His belly twitched from her touch as her fingers navigated their way downward.

She wasted no time with his pants. She'd undone the button and tugged the fly down in almost one single move. The next second she was attacking his pants, grasping them at the top and pulling them down. She slid his pants and underwear down in one quick motion, exposing him to her all at once. He lifted his butt at her urging and his cock sprang forth, standing proudly before her.

She pulled the pants down of his legs and dropped them to the floor. Her hands reached out to grasp his upper legs, asserting a gentle pressure on them. He opened his legs to, happy to oblige her insistence. Her hand came up to encircle his erection, with blue skin surrounding pink. He let out a moan as she grasped him.

"So beautiful and eager," she whispered.

He let his eyes half close as he enjoyed her attentions. She stroked his cock in slow, deliberate motions and teased the breath out of him. Then felt her move closer to him. He opened his eyes and saw her straddling him. Her crotch was so near his, her sex was almost touching him. Then with a slow movement, she eased herself against him, stroking her pussy against his cock. She repeated the motion, until his erection was slick with her ample wetness.

He could hear them both sigh as she slid over him and took him inside her. She pushed against him and took him all the way. He gasped as he felt her surrounding him and his cock strained against her warm embrace. She tensed her body and he felt her muscles grasp him tighter. She paused there and held onto his shoulders; she hesitated before moving her hips back. She pressed forward again and he met her motion, pushing against her. He let out his breath in a long slow exhale as he moved his body with hers.

Her pace quickened just slightly. Her hands held onto him tightly as he met her thrust for thrust. He brought his hands around her and they grabbed on, grasping her at the base of her back. He lifted his hips to join her and felt his feet flex as another bolt of pleasure shot through him. He grabbed her buttocks and pulled her against him. He let out another moan as he pumped into her.

His breathing sounded heavier in his ears as they worked away. He closed his eyes and concentrated on the tension slowly building within him. They pumped together again and another ripple of sensation flowed through him. He shivered as he felt his cock sliding into her. He could feel the energy building, but it was slow in coming. A mental pressure was building up within him more quickly, urging him for a release that was still distant.

His hands moved around her sides as he tried to guide her to his intentions. He held back. He stopped his thrusts against her and then pushing against her slowly. She looked at him, her eyes questioning his actions. Then as he moved, she understood. She let him up to stand above her while she laid down on the bed, and let her legs hang over the side. He reached down to grab her legs; he held them up while he positioned himself. Then with a quick motion, he was back inside her; they were joined again after the brief interlude.

He pushed into her, feeling her warmness surround him once more. He pumped his hips as the sensations played over him again. He could feel a small tingle in his crotch begin to grow and he picked up speed. The feel of her pussy stroking against his cock as he slid in and out of her stoked the need within him. She gripped then released him as she felt sparks of tension and pleasure dance through her body.

He looked down at her supine form and was struck by her beauty. She was laying there, her body stretched out before him. She had submitted herself to his pleasure, letting him take her as he pleased. This draconic beauty, this ancient goddess and his friend, was his patient and receptive lover. Her mouth was open and he could see her reptilian tongue poking out. He could see her breasts move slightly with the motion of their bodies.

That all spurred him on and he felt the need growing stronger within him. He held onto her legs tighter and pushed into her as he pumped his hips faster. He heard her moan as he changed the tempo and that tugged at his mind and sent another shiver through him. He felt her butt move as she lifted her hips to meet his motions. He grasped her legs and pushed harder. The tension inside him was growing tighter; he could feel the familiar itch building in his balls.

He pushed again and again as he continued to pump into her. He felt the manic desperation drive him on and he pushed his hips against hers. He watched as she lay there, with her eyes closed and tongue lolling out. Her body moved in time with his. He heard her gasp again and that was it; that pushed him over the edge. He gave one final frantic thrust into her and felt the knot within him tighten and release.

He stopped and his body arched as he felt his climax hit him. All the stress poured out of him. His vision blurred and he closed his eyes as the wonderful dizzy sensation hit him. He pressed against Ishandra's legs, leaning on them for

Will A. Sanborn

support as the spasms shook him. His body shivered and he let out a protracted gasp as he felt his cock spurting inside her.

And then it was over, the last quivers died down as he jerked his hips forward and tried to squeeze one last surge of pleasure from the fading climax. He stayed there, eyes closed, still leaning against her for balance, while he waited for his breathing to return to normal.

He slowly pulled out of her. He heard their mingled sighs once again as they plucked one another's now-sensitive skin. He then flopped down to join her on the bed, as that sudden sleepy feeling overcame him. He reached out for her and took her in embrace. The warmth of her body against his in the midst of the bliss of the tired afterglow felt so natural.

Moments or minutes passed while they lay together. His attention was eventually caught again when he felt her nuzzling her head against him. He opened his lazy eyes to see her smiling up at him. He reached up to stroke the top of her head, feeling her smooth skin beneath his fingers again. He gave her ear an idle touch and she smiled at him. He kissed the tip of her snout again and she let out a contented sigh.

"That was beautiful" she said. Her voice was low and dreamy.

He nodded, but then a concerned look came into his eyes. "I hope that wasn't too rushed..."

She chuckled at that. "Of course not, hon. I enjoyed the intensity of it. It felt like you could really use it too." He smiled and she continued, "that's good. I'm glad I could make you feel better, and it was fun having you work out all that tension that way."

"Thank you," he whispered.

"Of course," she added, as a smile starting to show on her own face, "if you'd like we can stretch things out the second time... I'm sure you could be in the mood for that." As she spoke he felt her hand trailing down his belly to come to rest on his crotch. The slow gentle strokes she gave him led him to agree that he'd probably be up for that.

Later, after their second bout of pleasure, they crawled under the covers to let sleep overtake them. As they slumbered, Thomas' dreams were uneasy. He did not wake from them though, instead he held onto Ishandra's body for comfort in his sleep, as the visions played on through his subconscious.

Will A. Sanborn

Chapter 8: Yet Another Revelation

Hang on St. Christopher through the smoke and the oil
Buckle down the rumble seat, let the radiator boil
Got an overhead downshift, and a two dollar grill
Got an 85 cabin, on an 85 hill
Hang on St. Christopher on the passenger side
Open it up tonight, the devil can ride
    Tom Waits, "Hang on St. Christopher"

I'm not the same man I was before
I haven't changed my perception
I haven't lost my protection
I haven't lost, haven't lost, haven't lost
What I have, lost intentions
    Oingo Boingo, "Same Man I Was Before"

It was nice to be able to wake up next to Ishandra the following morning. Thomas snuggled with her under the covers as they both came awake slowly. The strange quest they were on and the unknown danger that lay before them didn't feel quite as forbidding as he felt her warmth beside him. They spent a little more time living in the present and enjoying each other's presence, before they finally got up to get showered and dressed. When they met up with the others for breakfast, Thomas was in good spirits, ready to take on the new day and whatever lay ahead of them.

As it turned out, the trip that day was pretty much uneventful. The Rocky Mountains were behind them, so they were driving out across the plains, which weren't all that interesting to look at. After seeing the wide expanse of land for miles upon miles, it lost its interest pretty quickly. They made good time though, putting a good amount of distance behind them. They still weren't sure where they were going. The angel had not yet returned to give Mark any new information, and while Thoth could detect the growing magical presence, he couldn't tell how far away it was. He had a rough idea of their heading, but that was it. It was all they had to go on though, so they continued onward towards the unknown.

Anubis and Thoth had managed to fit in with the group well, and were acting right at home with Mark, Ishandra and Thomas. Thomas felt himself talking to the two of them more again that day, and they continued to indulge his questions about the way things had been in Egypt. Ishandra had told Thomas about her people and her goddess, but it didn't have as big an impact as Thoth and Anubis' tales. Theirs was a history Thomas had heard more about and he could relate to it better. He was also fascinated by the pantheon of gods they had, and didn't tire of hearing the different stories about all of them and their various exploits.

Anubis was more than happy to talk about the old times once again. He seemed flattered that Thomas was so interested about them. Thomas could see a growing interest in him from Anubis, but tried to disregard it; he found he was able to most of the time. If the jackal's attentions to him were more than just friendly, he kept them to himself and was a perfect gentleman. It still felt odd, but he had to smile about it the couple of times he let his mind wander to those thoughts. Ishandra was right, in a strange way, it did feel a little flattering. Anubis' personality was warm, and when he was happy his enthusiasm was infectious. The more he talked with the two of them, the more he found he liked them. Even Thoth had his own simple grace, in the quiet way he spoke. His intellect and knowledge were impressive, and occasionally he'd let his warmer side slip through his stoic demeanor.

◆ ◆ ◆

They stopped for dinner at a local establishment a ways off the beaten path. Mark complained that he was tired of eating in the generic highway restaurants and wanted to get some local color, to get back to the salt of the earth as it were. The place he chose was a small bar and grille, though it looked like the bar aspect of it got a lot more attention. Plus, it didn't look like the type of place that'd call itself a 'grille,' especially with that fancy spelling. It was just a local watering hole and a place to get some grub.

It looked kind of rustic as they drove in. Thomas' car didn't look at home with the rest of the vehicles in the parking lot. His sedan was lost in a sea of old Ford and Chevy pickup trucks. Mark had wanted an authentic dining experience, and it looked like this place was about as far away from the gentrified chain restaurants as you could get. Thomas was a little nervous as they walked into the smoky room. Some of the locals turned around to look at the newcomers and he could feel their eyes upon them as the patrons took in the sight of the motley crew which had just entered their realm.

Mark seemed confident though. He paid no head to the stares as they walked to an empty booth. He even gave Thomas a confident smile as they sat down. Thomas tried to relax a little. They were out of place, but they were a good-sized group. He had three immortals to back him up. Mark looked like he'd seen his fair share of fights in his life too, so he could probably handle any trouble that came their way as well. Thomas just hoped it wouldn't come to that.

The waitress came a few minutes later. She did a bit of a double-take when she saw them all, but she was very nice. "Ah, I see you all aren't from around here?" she asked. They shook their heads and Mark answered that no, they were just passing through. "Well, thanks for stopping by, hon" she said with a smile. She appeared amused by their group, but her hospitality seemed genuine.

Will A. Sanborn

Mark ordered a Jack Daniels and Coke to drink and Thomas and Ishandra both ordered a domestic beer. "Do you have any wine?" Anubis asked.

"Sorry hon, we don't get much call for that around here."

"No, okay, I should've realized that's a bit decadent. I'll take a beer then as well." The waitress' face darkened momentarily at his comment, but the jackal's sincere smile won her over. Thoth ordered a similar libation.

"This isn't a wine kind of establishment, Anubis old buddy" Mark said with a big grin after the waitress had left.

Anubis nodded. "I should've realized that. In Egypt it was reserved for the royalty. I see that's still the case, even if it's more common in this world now."

"You'd better watch what you say in here," Mark replied. His expression turned serious as he spoke.

"I meant no ill will by that," Anubis replied.

"Well, some of the folks might not take it that way."

That didn't help Thomas feel any more at ease, but as the minutes passed he found he was able to relax more. They got their drinks and ordered their food. He felt Ishandra's hand on his shoulder and when he looked up at her she just smiled. She guided him to lean against her and then he felt her arm around his chest, offering the comfort of her warmth. Thomas gave her a smile, and let himself relax against her. The beer helped settle his mood too. He was drinking it on an empty stomach, and he could feel its warmth spreading over him.

Ishandra had also reached out with her other hand, and had taken Mark's hand in hers as he sat on the other side of her. Anubis followed suit and leaned in closer to Thoth. All at once things seemed okay with the world, at least for that moment. Thomas looked out across the room and saw that a few of the patrons at other tables were still stealing looks in their direction. Most of the folks seemed amused by the sight though and appeared to be entertained by the curious newcomers. Thomas caught the eye of one man who gave him a smile and a knowing nod. Perhaps he wouldn't mind being the one curled up next to Ishandra. Thomas fought against his embarrassment and was able to return a polite nod.

The nice mood lasted for several more minutes. Their peace was eventually shattered by a rude interruption. "So, it looks like you guys are having fun" a cold voice blurted out. Thomas looked up to a young man in his early to mid-twenties standing next to their table, looking down on them with hard, cold eyes. He looked wiry and mean.

"Is there a problem?" Mark asked, his voice also sounding cool.

"Just you city folk who think you can come in here like fucking tourists" the man shot back.

"This doesn't look like an exclusive club. We have just as much right to be here as you do."

"Why don't you take your money elsewhere? We don't need you here. We especially don't need any freaks," their antagonist shot back as he motioned towards Anubis and Thoth as they leaned against each other. "Take that shit somewhere else."

Thomas sat up straight and gave a nervous glance around the room. He saw the people at the nearby tables were looking on. Their faces showed concern and embarrassed anger. They looked like they were holding back, to see where things would end up going.

"You talk a lot, but it doesn't look like you have much to back it up." Mark replied. His eyes were fixed tightly on the man now.

"Just get the hell out of here. We don't need your kind here."

"Be careful son, you don't want to get something started that you won't be able to finish... From what I can see, you're the only one with the problem. I don't see any friends backing you up."

The angry punk just looked at him; his eyes narrowed to focus on Mark. He didn't make any other moves for a couple of moments. Finally Mark stood up to face him. He got in very close until he was almost breathing down the younger man's neck. "Now listen here, son. I don't want any trouble, but you'll get it if you don't leave us alone. Just go back to your barstool and have another drink. Or better yet, take a walk on out of here."

Thoth stood up as well. Thomas might've risen to add his support, but it wasn't easy for him to do so as he was sitting on the inside end of the booth. Their adversary took a look at Mark; he stood a few inches over him and outweighed him by close to fifty pounds. His eyes widened as he glared at Mark, then his composure broke and fear was evident on his face.

He took a step back. He still glared at Mark, but the wind was falling out of his sails. He hesitated a few moments more. "Fuck you freaks! I don't want to be here with you around" he spat out and turned and walked away. He tried to keep the bravado in his swagger, but it was failing as he made it to the exit. The fact that the people at the nearby tables, who'd been watching the events unfold, started to laugh at his retreat didn't help his cause any.

After the punk was gone, a couple of people came over to introduce themselves to the group. "Good job on that little shit" one man said as he shook Mark's hand. Some drinks were exchanged and Mark really seemed to be in his element. Thomas felt shaken, but as things died down he was able to relax a little more once again. At least the rest of the patrons in the bar were friendly, and with Mark having impressed them, it didn't look like there'd be any other problems that night.

They got their food and had a good meal, and after an hour the incident was all but forgotten. It seemed more like a distant memory as they enjoyed their dinner. Finally it was time to leave though. They said good-bye to their new friends and headed out to get back on the road and find a hotel for the night.

The parking lot was poorly lit, with only one street light at the far end of it, and the lights from the bar, but it was enough to see to get around in. They walked to the car with the afterglow of a good meal and the warm atmosphere of the place staying with them. Thomas' car was easy to spot amongst the trucks

Will A. Sanborn

and he took the keys from Mark. Mark had taken a few drinks and he wasn't in the best shape to drive. He was getting around okay, but his reflexes seemed a little dulled. Thomas had seen this early on, and had switched to soft drinks so he'd be able to drive.

Thomas was opening the door when he heard a sound off to the side, and in front of him. As he turned, he saw the punk from earlier in the evening was coming around the front of the truck next to them. "Nobody makes a fool out of me!" he yelped at them, and even in the low light Thomas could see the mad spark of anger in his eyes. An instant later he saw that the guy had a knife in his hand; he was bringing it forward, getting ready to use it.

Before he had a chance to react, Thomas felt a strong arm grab him and pull him back. He lost his footing and fell backwards as Mark pushed his way in front of him. It all happened so fast. Thomas fell down upon the gravel and Mark was in front of him in an instant, placing himself between the madman and the rest of them. Their attacker's mouth twisted into a wild grin when he saw Mark step into the fray.

Thomas' feet kicked out from under him and in doing so they caught Mark's foot as he stepped forward. Mark stumbled, he didn't lose his balance completely, but it was enough to lose his advantage. He went to grab the knife from the wild man's hand, but his missed. That was all the advantage the man needed, and as Mark's hand shot past his and failed to connect, the attacker brought his arm up. Mark was unable to block it and the knife made contact with him; its blade slid into his gut with a wet tearing sound.

Thomas saw it all from his vantage point on the ground. He couldn't help not seeing it as he looked up and helplessly watched the man attacking Mark. Mark let out a guttural groan and doubled over. Blood started to flow from the wound, pooling around the knife blade and soaking through Mark's shirt.

Their assailant gave the knife a twist in Mark's belly, making the wound bigger. His wild grin had gotten bigger and his eyes shone like a madman. "Who's the big man now?" he cackled as he gave the blade another shove.

Mark let out another wretched groan, but even as he did so his hand reached out to grab for the knife. He clasped his fist over the other man's hand, holding it firmly. With a Herculean effort, he straightened himself up and let another moan escape his mouth as he did so. He kept his grasp firmly on the knife handle, and as he stood up he summoned the strength to squeeze his fist down on his attacker's hand.

The other man let out a gasp of surprise as Mark tightened his grip. Then Mark twisted the knife out of his grasp. He let out another cry as he did that, but he would not be deterred. He slowly extracted the blade from the savage wound in his stomach and held it up to his attacker. The assailant's face went pale; his mouth hung open as he saw Mark brandishing the weapon at him, which dripped with his own blood.

"I told you that you didn't want to start something you wouldn't be able to finish..." Mark uttered the words through his labored breathing. His eyes were lit up with determination and a rage just barely restrained. He held the bloody knife in front of the other man's face for several seconds. He watched him trembling in anticipation, and then Mark tossed it off into the weeds beyond the parking lot. "Get the hell out of here!" he finally managed to say through gritted teeth.

Stripped off all his bravado once again, their assailant took one more look at the wild expression on Mark's face and the open wound in his belly, and then he took off. He scrambled away, out of the parking lot and didn't stop running even when he reached the road.

Thomas felt hands reaching down for him. He looked up and saw it was Anubis lifting him up. Thoth and Ishandra were stuck behind them, unable to get between Thomas' car and the truck next to it. Thomas saw the shock on all of their faces as he glanced back at them, though he briefly noted that Ishandra didn't look as afraid as the two Egyptians. He then turned his attention to Mark. "Oh shit" he heard himself say.

Mark had turned around to face them. His hands had gone to his stomach; he clutched the evil wound and gritted his teeth as the pain overwhelmed him. "Damn that hurts" he said through his halted breathing. In Thomas' state of shock, the quick thought struck him that it was an unfortunate choice of last words. Then his old training from first-aid classes kicked in.

Thomas thrust his hand down upon Mark's, adding more pressure to cover the wound and to try and stop the flow of blood. He turned back to his other three companions and barked orders at them. "Quick, we need to get something to make bandages out of, some heavy fabric, and something to tape them up with. Somebody run back inside and get help..."

Mark shook his head. "That won't be necessary, Thomas." Mark's words were less labored now, but they still sounded pained. Thomas stared at him in disbelief. Glancing backwards he saw that Ishandra had grabbed hold of Thoth's hand and was motioning for both he and Anubis to stay there.

"It's okay" he heard Ishandra say as he looked at the dragoness for support.

"She's right," Mark said, and his breathing was returning to normal. "You can take your hand away now." When Thomas made no move, Mark pushed his hands away to reveal the wound again. As Thomas looked at it, it appeared smaller than before. A second later he realized it was no longer bleeding as well. Then, just as when Ishandra had cut herself as a demonstration, he could see the wound reversing.

He stared in disbelief and watched the flesh knit itself back together. Without even realizing it, he took a step back from Mark. He moved back again as the tissue closed over the shrinking opening, finally leaving unbroken skin, unmarred by even the faintest scar. Thomas continued to back away from Mark until he bumped into Anubis. He stopped as he felt the jackal's hands coming up to rest on his shoulders, steadying him.

Will A. Sanborn

"Take it easy, Thomas" Mark said, his voice having returned to normal. "I know this is a shock to you, but I'll explain it all." He paused, and then added "I guess you can see now that I'm immortal too."

Thomas continued to stare at him and he felt his body shudder from the shock. Mark's face had become calm and stoic again, and the wound had vanished. His clothes still bore the mark of the savage attack though. His shirt and the front of his pants were stained with the blood which was seeping its way into the fabric. Thomas glanced back and saw that both Thoth and Anubis looked shocked as well. Ishandra had her head lowered just slightly, her eyes showing regret.

"We shouldn't wait around here though" Mark continued. "I don't know if our friend might decide to come back, and maybe bring some people with him. We don't want anyone inside coming out to see this either... It'd be much better if we got out of here and didn't get tangled up with talking to the police."

It didn't take much convincing for Thomas to realize that would be a good idea. Even with the sudden wariness he felt towards Mark, he agreed with the man's suggestion. They all hurried into the car and made it away from the scene. Thomas had to keep reminding himself not to drive too fast, to keep it under control. The last thing they wanted to do was to get stopped for speeding.

◆ ◆ ◆

"Okay, I guess it's time I told you about me" Mark spoke from the back seat as they drove along. "You know I'm an immortal too, but I'm not a god, Thomas. I know I probably should've told you earlier, but there was already so much for you to take. I'm sorry that you had to find out about it the hard way though. You've already been through so much." Thomas couldn't think of how to respond to that, he barely knew how to feel. He felt Ishandra's hand rest on his leg as a show of support. He appreciated the gesture, but at the same time he felt resentment towards both of them boiling up within him. He was glad that it was night out, so they couldn't see his face in the dark.

Mark continued his explanation. "It was a long time ago, back when the west was open. I was at a bar not too unlike the one we were just at, though the clientele were a good deal rougher. I'd been drinking and playing poker. There was a disagreement over something in the game, I can't remember what it was now, but we got into a fight. Things turned bad, and I got shot in the gut. Then, even as I was fading, they dragged me out into a back room to let me die."

"I remember lying there, feeling my breaths get shorter as the pain in my gut grew cold and dull. My last thoughts were that of how useless it was to get shot down like that, to die over a stupid game of cards and some lost wages. And then it hit me, I wasn't feeling sorry for myself, I was feeling regret for all the pain and suffering I'd caused, all the people I'd hurt. I wished I could take it back, not in trying to get into Heaven, I'd resigned myself to Hell for the life I'd led, but I wished I could've made a difference." Thomas listened in silence, but was struck by the similarities between Mark's tale and what had just happened.

He felt another shiver run through him as he envisioned the attack and Mark's wound all over again.

"Then, while I was lying there mourning the loss of a wasted life," Mark continued, "and feeling the strength drain out of me as my blood pooled on the floor, she was there. I looked up and saw the angel, the one I told you about the other day, Thomas. She appeared to me, not in a dazzling radiance, but with a simple glow of grace about her. She asked me if I was serious in how I felt about wanting a second chance, and if it wasn't just a death bed recantation, because that wouldn't work."

"I told her yes, that I'd give anything to be able to make a change. I could feel the sorrow washing over me and I didn't want to spend eternity stuck in that state, with my regrets my only company. She said that God had need of men like me on occasion and if I'd give over my life to Him, then He could grant me my second chance. I agreed without really knowing the full extent of what I was doing, but if I had to do it all over again, I'd still place my life in His hands like I did that night."

"'Then let His grace save you,' she said and she knelt down to touch my wound. I felt a burning heat as soon as she touched me. It was almost too much to take, but then as it radiated through me, I felt the warmth of the power that saved my life. Then my wound was healed and the pain was gone. She helped me stand up and told me that my life was saved and that it would be different now, that I was to live my life for Him."

"Well, it had quite an impact on me, at first. I was shaken up and I walked the straight and narrow, for awhile. I tried to change, but old habits die hard. As the months passed I fell back into my vices. It was a year or two later when I found myself in another fight. This one guy pulled a knife on me. He didn't get in a fatal blow like the first time, or our friend tonight, but he did cut me pretty bad. It was when I saw and felt the cut heal itself that the true nature of my salvation was revealed. It sure scared the hell out of the guy I was fighting with too. He turned as pale as a ghost and ran away screaming." Another shudder gripped Thomas as he heard history repeating itself. He kept quiet as he listened to Mark's tale. The other members of their party were silent as they listened on as well.

"That was a lot for me to take though and I wandered out into the desert night to try and get my thoughts straight. After a couple of hours of thinking on my own, I ran across the angel once again. She looked both sad and concerned as she told me about the gift that'd been bestowed upon me. God had not only saved my life, but he had made me immortal. That was not done so I could continue to waste my life though. I'd been given this chance to turn things around and I hadn't done that yet. I was to make something better of the new life given to me. I was to try and help people. She also said that there'd be times in the future when they'd call on me to help them out, and they hoped I would do so. She told me that she hoped I would do something with this wonderful chance that had been given to me."

"Well at first I was scared, and then I was angry" Mark continued. "How dare God do that to me? I didn't want to have to roam the earth like that forever. It took months before I could reconcile it all, and finally see it as the gift it really was. Sure there was a twist to it, but as they say, He does work in mysterious ways. I'd asked for a second chance, and I was given a whopper of one. It took me even longer to turn my life around, but I was able to do it. It was hard, and I never did give up all of my vices. I don't believe He expected me to though, nor do I think it was really required. Instead I tried to change who I was and how I behaved towards people. I tried to make a difference where I could, and to help those I was able to. I haven't been a saint, but I'm a lot less of a sinner than I once was. His grace has helped me with that, and it helped me come to terms with how my life is now. He really did save my life."

"I've seen a lot of changes since then, and there've been tough times, but the faith I have in His grace has kept me going all these years. He's showed me where I could help people, but also showed me how to find solace in this world. I believe He led me to Ishandra too. Now you can see why I care so much about her, Thomas, and why we're together even if our relationship isn't a conventional one. We've both helped each other out a lot." As he said that, Ishandra reached back to take his hand.

"So you've been helping people out all this time, for all these years?" Thomas asked. His voice sounded unsteady.

"Yes, not all of the time of course. I help out when I can, where I see a need. The carnival has worked well for that. We go around from town to town, and sometimes I see a place where I can make a difference and I do it. I've tried to help some of the people in the carnival find religious inspiration if it looks like they need it too. The angel has come to me a few times over the years with tasks as well. This quest is by far the biggest one that's been set before me though."

Thomas didn't know how to respond, so he kept quiet. Nobody else decided to break the silence, so they drove along without saying anything more until they found a hotel to pull into for the night.

◆ ◆ ◆

Mark didn't say anything to Thomas as they unloaded their bags from the car. Thomas was too numb to care about talking with him at the moment, so he just hurried to the room. Ishandra followed him there.

"Thomas, are you okay?"

"I don't know... You should've told me, Ishandra, you both should have."

"I know. I'm sorry. At the time we thought it'd be easier for you if we didn't have to show you everything at once. Believe me that we didn't know you'd find about it the way you did tonight." She reached out to hug him and he didn't resist. She still felt warm, but his thoughts were in turmoil.

"Can you forgive me, hon?"

He pulled back to look at her. He felt his eyes watering as he spoke. "I'll try, Ishandra, but it's a lot to deal with right now. I don't hate you for it, but I still feel betrayed."

She was silent as she looked back at him and then leaned her head against his shoulder. "I'm sorry" she whispered.

They stayed like that for several minutes, just holding onto one another. It was the dragoness who broke the silence. "Do you want me to stay with you tonight?" Her eyes were wet as well as she studied him.

Thomas felt the conflict rising up inside him. He hesitated, and then finally shook his head. "I think I need to be alone tonight, Ishandra. I'm not pushing you away, but I need some time to think."

She gave him a solemn nod. "I can understand that Thomas. Please come to get me if you change your mind and you need to talk though."

They hugged again, this time only briefly though. "Be well, I'm worried about you," she said as she planted a soft kiss on his forehead.

"I'll try" he managed to reply, his voice low. "We can talk more tomorrow." He watched her leave the room, then locked the door behind her. He immediately regretted turning her away like that, but at the same time the feeling of betrayal nagged at him. He didn't want that turning his affections for Ishandra sour, especially if she was with him at the time.

A few minutes later as he was brushing his teeth, the need to talk to someone overwhelmed him. He realized he wouldn't be able to get to sleep if he didn't have someone to discuss things with. He hesitated as he considered his options. He could go and get Ishandra, but he still thought it would be better to keep his distance from her, at least for the night. He was a little wary of seeing Mark again that evening as well. Finally he realized his only option was to talk to his new friends, the Egyptians.

He'd knocked on their door before he realized that they might already be in bed. They could also be spending some quality time together. He blushed as he realized that and almost wanted to slink away from the door before he could interrupt them. The door was opened a moment later, before he could get away, and he was greeted by Thoth.

"Thomas is something wrong?" the ibis asked as he cocked his head and looked at him.

"Uh, I just needed someone to talk to... is that okay?"

Anubis joined Thoth in the doorway. "Of course Thomas, I think I know what this is about."

They let him into the room and moved back to sit on the bed. Thomas decided to sit on the floor with his back against the bed. That gave something to lean back against and it also meant he didn't have to look directly at either of them.

"You had quite a shock tonight" Anubis said. "We all did."

"Neither of you knew about Mark? Not even you Thoth?"

The ibis shook his head. "No, I got a sense that something was different about him, but I couldn't tell what it was. He definitely wasn't a god, I could tell that much, but I didn't know that he was immortal."

"Why is it so hard for you guys to tell what's going on?" Thomas asked; his voice betrayed his frustration.

"The magic isn't as strong as it used to be, Thomas" Thoth said, and his voice was a little softer. "We can't do as much as we used to. I'm sorry..."

"I don't know how much more of this I can take. I mean we don't know what we're doing, where we're going, or even what exactly it is we're going to be dealing with. And to top it off, I'm the only one among us who can be hurt. I thought Mark was at least like me in that way, now I find out he's more like you..."

"I know you're feeling vulnerable..." Thoth started to say, but his words trailed off. He appeared lost for what to say next.

"Shush," Thomas heard Anubis say, "you've got the four of us here to protect you. From the looks of things Ishandra cares about you very much, and I doubt she or Mark would let anything happen to you. Thoth and I would do whatever we could to keep any harm from befalling you too."

"I just feel so lost in this."

"We're not so different, hon. We may be more permanent, but we're still just flesh and blood, like you." Thomas felt Anubis' hands reach down to rest on his shoulders. He didn't resist the gesture of care and affection. He just closed his eyes and let out a sigh instead.

He almost felt like crying, but the tears wouldn't come, so he sat there relaxed at the affirming touch of the jackal's hands. He gave a small whimper as he felt Anubis kneading the sensitive flesh of his neck with gentle deftness. He surrendered himself to the healing touch and let the stress melt away from him.

He was lost in the release for several long minutes, until he realized what was going on. A shiver ran through him as the rational side of his brain asserted itself once again. He turned to look up at the jackal. "Anubis, what are your intentions?" The tone of his voice filled in the question that he didn't speak.

Anubis stopped the gentle massage, but he did not remove his hands from Thomas' shoulders. "If you're worried I'm going to take advantage of you, you don't need to. I would never do that."

"But you want to...?"

"Yes, but not like this. Not with someone who wasn't willing."

Thomas looked up at him, but did not say anything.

"I am attracted to you, Thomas, in both body and spirit, but unless I have misunderstood things, I don't think you're one who's interested in the company of males."

Thomas shook his head. "It's never something I've considered." He then had a flash of the memory of his brief experimentations with his cousin so long ago, but he forced that down. "I've always been attracted to women."

"I saw you were sharing Ishandra's attention with Mark, so I thought that was the case. That's why I haven't been trying to get with you, no matter how cute I think you are."

"You're very lucky to be with Ishandra" he heard Thoth say. "She's quite beautiful."

"Does it bother you that I find you attractive?" Anubis asked.

"I don't know. It's never something I've had to think about. I guess I'm flattered, but it's still a little weird for me... I'm sorry."

"You don't need to apologize, hon."

"Thank you."

"You're welcome, and I think you're handling all of this quite well."

Thomas felt a warm glow spreading over him from the jackal's words. He looked up at Anubis and gave him a smile. His eyes had started to water again, but emotion felt good this time. "It's been so much to take, but I guess after awhile I just have to accept things as they come up and deal with them."

"You've got a very strong spirit, Thomas. You're one of the stronger humans I've gotten to know. Even some of my consorts couldn't stand up to everything that you've been through in these past couple of days."

"Your consorts?"

Anubis let out a nervous little chuckle. "Yes, I had human consorts from time to time, but I don't know if you'd want to hear about that."

"Well if you put it that way, now you have to tell me," Thomas replied with a smile, his interest piqued.

Anubis returned his smile and gave him a wink. "Back in the old days, when our dynasty was still in power, we were able to mingle with the mortals on occasion. There were times when we could take humans as consorts, lovers. I took my share of attractive males and shared many pleasures with them, for a time, before they were returned back to live out their lives. I have had dalliances with those in the afterlife too, though it was not as exciting for me as being with humans who had not yet experienced the world beyond the veil." A faraway look crept into the jackal's eyes as he spoke.

"It sounds like you liked a bit of adoration and hero worship," Thomas said with a grin.

Anubis chuckled once more. "Partly so, but it was also seeing how the experience affected them and how emotional it was. Humanity has always been so vital, and I loved to experience it all through them. I was careful in whom I chose though, and I made sure that those I did choose enjoyed the experience. I believe we both got a lot out of it." He paused then added, "I miss how that felt."

"But wasn't that a conflict of interest? I mean didn't you judge the souls of people as they were trying to get into the afterlife? Wouldn't you be temped to go easy on those who'd been your lovers?"

"I wasn't the judge, I was the officiator. The scales did all of the work, weighing their heart against the feather of truth. Besides, Thoth was there working along side of me, so he'd keep me honest." Anubis flashed a smile at his companion, and the ibis winked back at him.

"And you didn't mind his dalliances?" Thomas asked Thoth.

"Not in the least, Thomas." Thoth replied. "It might be hard for you to understand, but it didn't work the way you're used to. It's like the situation Mark and Ishandra appear to have. Our lives are different than yours, the longevity probably accounts for that. Anubis and I have been friends and lovers for a long time, but we've both taken other lovers at times. I haven't had as many as Anubis, but I've taken them when the need was there. For one thing, I've enjoyed females on occasion, unlike Anubis..." He winked at is his partner as he said that. Anubis just smiled and gave him a playful swat on the hand.

Thomas smiled at their antics, the two of them fit together so well. He still felt uncertainty nipping at him though. "It still sounds so strange. Can you really love that many people?"

"Do you care about Ishandra?" Thoth asked him.

"Well yeah, but I can't say I love her yet... It hasn't been long enough."

"But you enjoy the time you can spend with her?"

"Yes, that's true." Thomas felt the sting of her betrayal jump out at him again as he said that.

"So even if you don't end up spending your life with her, it's still something worthwhile that you shared?" Thomas had to nod in agreement at that and Thoth continued. "That's part of what it's like. It's possible to care about and love many different people in a lifetime, especially a long one. I know you're young and still finding things out for yourself, Thomas, but I hope that you'll get to experience many different connections with people that will be fulfilling. That's part of what makes life so worthwhile."

There wasn't much to talk about after that. Thomas felt tired from everything that'd happened that evening, but it had been good talking with Anubis and Thoth. Even if it raised some more questions; it just felt comfortable sitting in their presence and talking with them. He didn't want to return to his room alone, so he stayed there as long as he could, until fatigue was getting the better of him.

Finally it was time for him to say good-night. He thanked them both profusely for their help and his sentiments were genuine. He even surprised Anubis by given him a hug. He surprised himself a little at that too, but it just felt right. He embraced Thoth next and thanked the two of them again for taking the time to try and sooth his spirits.

He didn't want to leave, but he had to. When he returned to his empty room, he felt the solemn melancholy feeling seeping into him again. Thomas could never remember feeling so lonely before in his life as he lay there in bed, longing for sleep to come. As soon as the lights were out, his mind was a buzz with chaotic thoughts once more. The image of Mark getting stabbed replayed itself several times, and he felt the uneasiness creep over him.

He hugged the extra pillow against his chest and buried his head into it. His eyes were hot with tears once again. He felt the yearning in his heart for someone to share his bed, a warm body to help take away the pain. He thought of Ishandra, but then the sting of the secret she'd kept from him came up again. As he lay there, desperate for sleep to overtake him and craving companionship, the image of Anubis briefly flashed through his mind. That troubled him some too, but not as much as it might have. Finally, after tossing around in bed for the longest time, he fell into a fitful sleep.

Will A. Sanborn

Will A. Sanborn

Chapter 9: Time out for Fun

The walls are built up stone by stone, the fields divided one by one
And the train conductor says take a break driver 8, driver 8 take a break
We've been on this shift too long
And the train conductor says take a break driver 8, driver 8 take a break
We can reach our destination, but we're still a ways away
  R.E.M., "Driver 8"

Thomas felt horrible when he woke up the next morning. He hadn't slept too well the night before. His troubled thoughts had kept tugging at his mind, keeping sleep at bay. He'd finally fell into a fitful sleep, but then had woken up early in the morning with the first light of the day. He groaned and looked at the clock. It was too early to get out of bed, it was probably an hour before the rest of the group would be up, and so there was nothing to do but lie there and mull things over in his mind once again.

He stayed like that for about forty-five minutes, before he finally gave up and dragged himself out of bed. He was weary from the lack of sleep and his head hurt. He stayed in the shower for longer than usual, but even the warm water flowing over him didn't do much to help him feel better, or ease his mind. It was something to do though, and it offered a slight distraction.

When he was finally dressed, he figured it was time that the others would be up and about. The hurt and confusion from the night before still ate at him; it left a dull ache in his stomach. He paused at the door to Mark and Ishandra's room. They should be up by then, but would they be dressed and ready to go? He didn't want to bug them at an inopportune time. He thought about how Mark had surprised him and Ishandra when they'd first met. It had only been a few days ago, but it already felt like half a lifetime away; so much had happened.

He gave the door a hesitant knock. At least if they weren't ready, they didn't have to answer it. He listened for signs of life and felt his nerves go into overdrive as he waited. It was only a few moments, but it felt like more than that. Finally he heard someone padding across the carpet and then the dim light behind the eye-hole went dark. A moment later Ishandra opened the door to look out at him.

"Thomas, you look miserable" she said. Her voice was concerned, not critical.

"I didn't sleep too well," he answered, his voice sounding flat and tired. "We need to talk, can I come in?" He paused, and then added "are you guys dressed?"

"Almost," he heard Mark's voice answer back from inside "come on in, Thomas."

Ishandra opened the door wider and he stepped in, after a slight hesitation. He glanced behind the dragoness and saw that Mark was wearing a shirt and in the process of putting on his pants. A second later the older man was fully dressed, save for his shoes.

"Thomas, I'm sorry for all of this, we both are" Ishandra told him. She gave him a sad look as she said that.

"You should've told me about it earlier."

Ishandra cast her gaze down slightly and shook her head. "I know, hon. I was trying to protect you, but I ended up hurting you so much more than if we'd told you everything in the beginning."

"It's as much my fault, Thomas" Mark said. "I was afraid we'd freak you out even more if you knew about me from the beginning. Finding out about Ishandra and my talk with the angel was enough to throw you for a loop."

"But you've had long enough since then to tell me."

"I know," Mark answered, and his voice sounded just a little weary too. "But it got to the point that once we didn't tell you in the beginning, it seemed harder to reveal it later on, for just this reason... Even though it wasn't fair to you, I was wondering if we might be able to not have to let you know."

"The last thing we wanted to do was hurt you," Ishandra said as she offered Thomas her hand. He paused, and then took hold of it. The feel of her touch and the gesture of that simple act did warm him a little bit. "Can you forgive us?" the dragoness asked as she stared at him.

"I'm trying to" he replied as he felt his throat tightening. "Don't hold any more secrets from me, okay?"

She nodded and her expression brightened slightly. He looked over at Mark and he was nodding as well. The older man's look was still stoic though, which was the norm for him.

"I mean it," Thomas said. "Is there anything else you haven't told me about?" Both of them shook their heads at that. "Do you know what we're up against yet? Mark, have you heard anything more from the angel, has she returned to tell you more about what this is all about."

"No she hasn't. I guess it's not the time for that yet, son. Perhaps we aren't ready to know more about it."

Thomas shook his head and gritted his teeth. He then focused his attention back to Ishandra. "Have you been able to figure anything about it?"

She too shook her head. "No, I've tried one divination, but it didn't show anything. The events surrounding that unknown are still clouded. I'm going to try again when we get closer."

"Thoth doesn't know any more about it either."

She didn't look surprised to hear that. "I'm hoping that as we draw nearer, we'll be able to find out more." She paused, and then added "it's frustrating for me too, hon. I wouldn't realize it under most circumstances, but this is really showing how much my abilities have faded with the years."

He gave her hand a squeeze, but said nothing.

"I can promise you this though, whenever I do find something out, and whatever it is, I will tell you." She looked into his eyes as she said that, and she squeezed his hand in return.

He gave her a silent nod. He still felt weary, but he could feel his trust slowly returning.

"Will you be okay with all of this, Thomas?" Mark asked a few moments later.

"I think so," Thomas replied. "I'll try." As Thomas looked at him, he could see he was the same man he'd known all along, no matter what had been revealed. He still felt apart from the rest of the group, and that was something he'd have to reconcile. They felt like friends after the days they'd spent together on the road, so that helped, no matter how different they might be.

"You're not alone in this, hon" he heard Ishandra say to him.

"Yes, we're all here to help you if you need it" Mark added. A few seconds later, he offered another bit of assistance. "Thomas, would you like to pray with us for help along this journey?"

"I don't know, I still don't know what I believe..."

"It can't hurt, and it can help if you open yourself up to the possibilities."

Thomas glanced at Ishandra, "do you pray with him too?"

She nodded. "When times call for it, yes."

"But how, how can you pray to that God?"

Mark cracked a slight smile. "I believe God is a lot more open to things than what some people might say. If you open yourself to Him, then He'll welcome you."

"Okay, I'll try" Thomas said as he took Mark's hand and the three of them formed a small circle.

They bowed their heads and closed their eyes and Mark started to talk in a soft voice. "God above us, please look down and help us, Your humble servants, as we continue along on this task You've set before us. Help us to find the way and to be able to do what is required of us. Please help us all find the peace of understanding, whatever ways we can."

As they stood there and he listened to Mark's words, Thomas felt a little better. It didn't seem spiritual, but sharing the moment of silence and peace with the two of them helped to lift his mood, if only slightly.

"Thanks" he whispered to Mark when they were finished.

"Thank you for giving it a chance" Mark replied.

After breakfast it was time to pile into the car once again for another day of driving. Mark told Thomas that he looked much too wiped out to drive, and said that he should try and get some rest. Thomas rode in back between Anubis and Ishandra, and took Ishandra up on her offer to lean against her. She put her arm around him and he relaxed against her. He felt Anubis give his arm a quick pat as a show of support as well. He turned his head to give the jackal a nod of thanks before he closed his eyes and tried to find sleep.

Sleep was not elusive as it had been the night before, and he was soon lost in the bliss of a pleasant nap. He had no dreams, no troubled thoughts; it was just a chance for his mind to go dormant and his body to relax. Some time later he came awake, bit by bit to find himself still in Ishandra's arms. He gave a happy sigh as he leaned against her and didn't make any moves to sit up. He was quite content to stay where he was.

"Feeling better?" she asked him.

"Yes, thank you."

"Good, then you can take over driving soon" He heard Mark's voice from the driver's seat and Thomas looked up to see him smiling at him.

"No rest for the weary?" Thomas shot back at him, feeling his own smile creep across his face.

"Something like that" Mark returned with a bit of a chuckle.

Mark actually gave him longer than that to rest and relax, and Thomas didn't take over driving until after lunch. The afternoon's drive was uneventful, and more of the same. The plains and flat countryside of the Midwest didn't change all that much. Somewhere in Minnesota, Thoth broke the monotony though.

"We're definitely getting closer," the ibis god said. Thomas gave him a quick questioning glance, and then turned his eyes back to the road. "The force that's out there, whatever it is, I can feel it getting stronger now. It's gotten noticeably stronger since this morning."

"Can you tell anything more about it?" Mask asked.

"No, still not yet, but I can feel it growing."

An hour or so later Thoth remarked that he felt it increasing more. Thomas saw the road sign for Minneapolis and St. Paul only fifty miles away. "Do you think it could be there?" he asked as he pointed it out.

"It could be likely, anything is possible."

They continued to drive on. It was early in the evening as they were approaching the Twin Cities. They were still out in the suburbs when Thomas saw another sign which caught his interest. Without bothering to consult the others, he turned off at the next exit.

"Where are you going?" he heard Ishandra ask him.

"I decided to take a little detour. We're going to stop at the mall?"

"The mall?" Mark asked. His voice sounded dubious.

"Yes, but it's not just any mall, it's the 'Mall of America'" Thomas said, as he added a bit of dramatic flare to his voice.

"You can't be serious?"

"Hey, it's something that always sounded amusing for how ridiculous it was. Besides, it's my turn to pick where we have dinner." He grinned as he said that,

Will A. Sanborn

even though his passengers in the back seat couldn't see his expression that well.

He thought about it, and then added "we don't know what we're likely to find as we get closer to whatever it is that Thoth is detecting. If we could be in danger, at least we can do something fun tonight." Thomas immediately realized how crazy and lame that sounded, but he forced himself to ignore it. "Who knows when I'll be out this way again anyway" he added and he heard no further dissention from the ranks.

They all let out a gasp of surprise in spite of themselves when they saw it. It's one thing to go to a mall, even a large one, but this structure was gigantic. It sprawled out over the landscape like the Emerald City. It was starting to get dark so the lights were coming on and it was lit up like a neon monstrosity, the Mecca of commerce and entertainment.

"You wanted to know more about our culture Anubis, well there it is, kitsch personified" Thomas said as they were getting out of the car. The jackal returned his smile as they both looked upon the radiance of American consumerism gone out of bounds.

"This should be interesting" Thoth added, and the sound of his voice got both Thomas and Anubis chuckling.

Even Mark cracked a smile. "Good idea, son" he said as he clapped Thomas on the shoulder. "I think we could all use a bit of absurdity right now."

And so they ventured on into the expanse of the mall, and tried to leave their worries about the outside world behind them for a couple of hours. Thomas was having a great time and he felt a bit like being a kid again. Of course it was silly to feel so excited about something so ridiculous, but it really didn't matter. It was fun because of the absurdity of it all, and Thomas enjoyed sharing the experience with his friends, who were also enjoying it in spite of themselves.

He split his time between Mark and Ishandra and Thoth and Anubis. Mark kept on shaking his head at the place, but Thomas caught him smiling every once in awhile. Ishandra told Thomas that it was good to see him smile. Thoth seemed intrigued by the commercial crassness of it all, and the sheer scale of everything. Anubis on the other hand was delighted at all of the people there. He looked happy as he went about people-watching. He also seemed a little more at home in a place where there were some exotics around; that way he, Thoth and Ishandra didn't stand out as much.

They'd ducked into a learning store for a bit, and before Thomas could realize it, they were standing in front of the section on ancient Egypt. At first Thoth and Anubis were interested when they saw the book on the mummies and the familiar face of the King Tut's ornate sarcophagus. However, they then came to a shelf of knick-knacks, such as tiny obsidian pyramids. Thomas saw Anubis looking at the little black figurines of cats and jackals. They were regular animals, not humanoid forms, but the reference was obvious. Before he could think to do anything, he saw Anubis' expression darken.

That Old Time Religion

Thoth noticed this as well and took the jackal's hand. "It's okay" he whispered, but he looked like he was lost for more words.

Anubis shook his head. "No it's not. This is all that's left... It's all gone, Thoth."

Thomas paused, trying to decide what to do, then went on impulse. He reached out to give a gentle touch to the Anubis' forearm. "I know the truth, Anubis" he whispered as he looked into the jackal's sad eyes. "At least somebody knows that you were really there and that you're still here..."

It was all he could think to say, but it seemed to help. Anubis gave him a solemn nod and then fought to regain his composure. They walked with him out of the store and when they reached the atrium he was acting a little better.

"Thank you, Thomas" Anubis said, "I really appreciate that."

"That was very thoughtful," Thoth agreed.

"You guys have made an impression on me, and I don't think I'm ever going to forget it." He almost wanted to add 'if I live to tell the tale, that is' as that thought crossed his mind, but he did his best to ignore it.

◆ ◆ ◆

When they came to the small amusement park in the center of the mall, Thomas had to work to get someone to go on the rides with him. He was really feeling like a kid at heart, and it was doing him good.

"I've had my fill of carnival rides," Mark said with a grin.

"I'd go, but it wouldn't work with my tail," was Ishandra's excuse. Thomas did have to agree with her that having such a long tail might not be that comfortable, and on a couple of rides it could end up being dangerous.

Thoth was acting too dignified to go on the rides, so Thomas turned to Anubis. "It looks like it's up to you then" he said with a smile. The jackal appeared a little dubious to the idea, but he went ahead with it on Thomas' insistence that he at least give it a try. Thomas got him on the roller coaster, the flume ride and the giant swings. Despite his misgivings, Anubis looked to be really enjoying himself. Thomas could feel the jackal's enthusiasm adding to his and it was also fun to see their three companions watching them with amused looks as they had their adventures.

Finally they were sated on the rides so they returned to join their friends. "Have you guys had enough yet?" Mark asked. "I'm getting hungry."

"Yes Dad," Thomas replied, and he saw the older man trying to hold back his smile at that. Thomas realized that he was getting hungry too, so dinner was definitely a good idea.

They passed up the glitz of Kokomo's Island Café to eat at the somewhat more respectable Twin City Grill. It was done up in the 1940's style and featured classic American cuisine. The understated atmosphere was good for them to relax, and the food was excellent. If not for the reason why they were on the road, the evening would've been perfect. Thomas caught himself thinking about that a couple of times, but then worked on distracting himself by

Will A. Sanborn

paying more attention to their dinner conversation. It felt good to be spending nice times with these new friends. After all the weeks before that he'd spent on the road mostly by himself, it was nice to have friendly and caring people around him.

♦ ♦ ♦

After dinner they decided they could take in one more attraction, so they finished off the evening by visiting Underwater Adventures. The giant aquarium was definitely worth checking out. It had some of the mall kitsch to it as well, but it offered many beautiful views of the undersea life. It was relaxing to watch the fish and turtles swim by in the giant tanks that surrounded them, and they spent a good time there soaking in the ambiance.

Thomas was walking next to Anubis as they were looking at the shark tank and decided to hang back. The others moved on ahead, he saw Thoth glance back at them and then continue on.

"Thanks for going on those rides with me earlier," Thomas said as he turned to look at Anubis.

"You're welcome, Thomas. It was fun."

"I wanted to thank you for last night too, for how you guys tried to make me feel better. I really appreciated that."

"It was the least we could do. I like you Thomas, and wanted to set you at ease in what ever capacity I could."

Thomas hesitated slightly, as doubts tried to creep back into his thoughts, but then he pushed onward. "I want to do something to thank you for how nice you've been to me..."

Anubis cocked his head slightly and raised one ear in curiosity. Thomas had to smile at that, as he was struck at how much the jackal's body language was a mix of human and animal.

"Would you like to spend the night together?" Thomas heard himself say. Even as he did it, he couldn't quite believe he'd actually spoken the words. He felt a shiver of nervous excitement go through him.

"Thomas...?" Anubis asked. His mouth hung open as he stared back at him.

"I think I'd like to try some things out..."

"Are you sure?"

"I think so. Yes. It still seems a little odd to think about, but you've got me wondering about things." Thomas bit his lip in an absent-minded reflex as he confessed his curiosity.

"You're not just doing this for me are you?" Anubis looked concerned.

"No, I have to admit I got curious about things once I got to thinking about it." Thomas hesitated, and then continued his explanation. "I did fool around a little bit with another guy, my cousin, when I was a teenager. We didn't do much, but it was enough to make me feel guilty later on. Maybe trying something out with you would show me I don't need to feel bad about it..."

That Old Time Religion

Anubis' ear twitched. "Very interesting" he said, almost to himself. He then addressed Thomas more directly "while I'd really like to play around with you Thomas, I don't want you to do anything that you'll regret later."

"I know it's quick, and I asked myself if it was just a reaction to everything, but it doesn't seem like that. I've been thinking it over and it intrigues me... I don't know how much I'd want to do, but I'd like to give it a try."

He looked at Anubis as the jackal was studying him and then added "and you are attractive and exotic, Anubis, I have realized that." He glanced around to make sure they were still alone in that corner of the aquarium, and then leaned in to give Anubis a kiss. It was quick and clumsy. For one thing he wasn't used to dealing with the jackal's muzzle, which was a bit different than Ishandra's snout. It got the point across though.

"Wow" Thomas heard himself say, and his voice had a hint of disbelief to it.

"I'll say that" Anubis responded.

"I hope that was okay."

"Yes, hon, I was just surprised that's all. You're really serious about this, aren't you?"

Thomas nodded. "With what we're facing, I figured it might not be bad to take a risk or two, for something that might be worthwhile to try out... Are you interested?" His voice betrayed the nervous feelings creeping over him, as he worried about the jackal's possible rejection."

Anubis dispelled that fear though. "Of course hon, if it's something you'd like. I'd love to spend the evening in your bed."

Thomas felt himself beginning to blush again, but he also smiled. "I think I'd really like that too."

"Well that's apparent." They both chuckled at that.

"It's okay if I don't want to do too much though, right? I'm not sure how far I want to go..."

"Of course, you're a friend, not a plaything. I'll be happy to enjoy whatever you feel comfortable in giving me, and if you change your mind about things, then I'll be okay with that too."

"Thank you for that." Thomas was starting to feel the warm glow of nerves and excitement mingling together within him. He paused, and then voiced his final point. "If it's okay with the two of you, I think I'd like to have Ishandra with us. We have a good connection that I'd like to keep open. I think she'd be a good for support and to help me if I get nervous..." Thomas then added "of course, I'd be focused on you."

Anubis' ears really perked up at that and Thomas saw his tail twitch. "My, you are full of surprises, Thomas. That's very playful and even a bit decadent, almost like a god. I'm impressed."

Thomas felt his smile grow wider as he looked at Anubis' happy and encouraging expression. "So you approve of that, then?"

The jackal gave him a silent nod of affirmation, and then leaned closer so their eyes met. Thomas saw those yellow eyes were radiating affection. The next

Will A. Sanborn

moment he felt Anubis' mouth making contact with his again. He closed his eyes and melted into the kiss. It was longer that time, and he felt a little more confident, but he still had to get used to it.

They heard a noise behind them and quickly broke off their kiss. They could hear some people coming down their way. They were hidden behind the curve of the tank, but only for the moment. If they dallied much longer they'd be discovered. So they moved apart and then headed down the hallway, going in the direction their friends had gone several minutes ago. Thomas gave a quick pat on Anubis' shoulder, and they both shared a secret smile as they walked away from the new group of people who were entering the shark-tank area.

When they rejoined their friends, Ishandra gave Thomas a slight smile and a questioning look, but both Mark and Thoth's expressions stayed neutral. Perhaps they wondered where the two boys had been, but they didn't make a point of it. Thomas was too excited to really care anyway. They were all friends and everyone had been very accepting of each other so far, so he saw no reason why that should change.

Thomas managed to pull Ishandra off to the side at the next available opportunity to tell her about what had happened between him and Anubis. Her response was very encouraging. "Very good Thomas. I was wondering if you'd do that, and I'm happy you have. I think it could be good for you."

"You knew?"

"You forget that I can pick up emotions, hon. It's something I can't help, so don't think I was snooping around on you. I got a feeling that you might be getting more than a little curious about him."

"Yeah, I still can't quite believe it, but I am intrigued by things, and he's got a really energetic personality."

"Well good for you, hon. I think you two will have fun."

"Uh, Ishandra, there's something I'd like to ask you?" Again he felt that anxious, awkward feeling creeping up on him, but he tried to push through it.

"Oh, what's that?"

"I'm still a little nervous about starting off things. I'm excited, but a little unsure. He's okay with that and won't push me into anything... But still, I'd like a little support. I know it's a little odd, but would you be okay with being there and helping me get over any stage fright?"

"Heh, I like that term for it" she let out with a giggle. "I'm really surprised at you, Thomas. You're really starting to blossom. We're having much more of an affect on you than I'd imagined. That sounds fun and I'd be proud to be with you for this and help you through it." She paused, then asked "Anubis is okay with that?"

"Yup, he seemed just as impressed as you."

"Well now, I think this could turn out to be very interesting indeed. Thank you for inviting me, Thomas."

He smiled at her and then took her hand and walked back to rejoin the others. He felt his excitement growing as tiny butterflies started to flap around in his stomach. Those nerves tickling his belly were good and welcome ones though. He felt like he was floating in a slight blissful daze. His thoughts still spun a bit, and it felt a little like being drunk. No mater what tomorrow might bring, tonight sounded like it would be an interesting diversion, one that he was definitely looking forward to.

Will A. Sanborn

Chapter 10: Trying it on the Other Side

If you change your mind, I'm the first in line
Honey I'm still free, take a chance on me
If you need me, let me know, gonna be around
If you've got no place to go, if you're feeling down
If you're all alone when the pretty birds have flown
Honey I'm still free, take a chance on me
Gonna do my very best and it ain't no lie
If you put me to the test, if you let me try
ABBA, "Take a Chance on Me"
(Covered by Erasure)

There is violet in the air tonight
I can see it on the road as we drive by
Everything I see is multiplied
On this sensory override
I can feel my inhibitions fade
And the fear has begun to give way
For the sun will shine another day
If I make it while I'm still sane
Mister Vertigo, "The Purple Song"

"Are you excited?" Ishandra asked Thomas as they waited in their hotel room for Anubis to join them.

Thomas gave her an uncertain nod. "Yeah, but I'm a little nervous too..." The initial euphoria had died down, and while he was still interested in spending the night with the jackal, some of his previous doubts had resurfaced.

"You'll do fine, hon" she said, as she gave him a hug. Her voice was soft and comforting. "You were all excited an hour ago, now you're just getting cold feet. You're doing a good thing here and you guys are going to have fun." She paused then whispered in his ear. "I'm really proud of you."

He smiled at her, feeling better and they shared a gentle kiss.

"Why don't I slip out of these clothes first?" she suggested. "That way we won't need to worry about that later."

He was all too eager to help. He reached up to undo the laces to her bodice, and then helped her with the buttons to her shirt. As that garment came off, he ran his hand along her belly and listened to the soft breath of air she exhaled. Her skirt was next; she let it drop to floor and stepped out of it, then stood before him in only her panties. Tonight her underwear was green; its fabric was a couple of shades lighter than her eyes.

She smiled at the approving look he gave her, and then made quick work of her panties as well. She slipped out of them with graceful ease. They joined the rest of her clothes on the small pile on the floor and she stood there in all her splendor before him once again. He felt his arousal growing and almost forgot who else was joining them. He started to tug on his shirt, working to get it untucked from his pants.

She reached out to touch his hand. "No, let Anubis help you get undressed..."

He gave her a sheepish look, but nodded and smiled. Just then there was a knock at the door. Ishandra smiled and gestured for him to open it, while she went to lie down on the bed. Thomas opened the door to reveal Anubis standing there. When he saw Thomas, his ears perked up.

"Hi again, sweetie" the jackal said as he entered the room and caught Thomas up in a hug that was warm and very close. Thomas reacted immediately, and his interests in Anubis came back to him. He wrapped his arms around the jackal and returned the embrace. The door shut behind them with a loud thud, but neither of them paid any heed to it, nor worried about annoying their neighbors with the noise. Thomas closed his eyes and sighed, as he remembered their little exchange back at the aquarium. Anubis felt very warm as he pressed his body against Thomas.

They eased off on the embrace and Thomas guided Anubis closer to the bed. When the jackal saw the nude dragoness lying on the bed watching them, he gave pause.

"Hello, Anubis" Ishandra said as she grinned at him. "I hope you don't mind that I got ready ahead of time. I wanted you and Thomas to focus on each other..."

He flicked one of his ears at her in amusement. "No that's quite alright, just a little surprising is all." He returned her smile. "While you're not my type, I can see why Thomas and Mark are so attracted to you. I can still appreciate beauty, wherever it may be."

"You're very good at flattery. You're quite handsome yourself" she said as she gave him a wink. "If you were interested, I'd be willing to spend some nights with you."

"Ah, but it's Thomas who I'm interested in, Ishandra, and I'm so happy that he's found an interest in me." Anubis squeezed Thomas' hand as he said that. He then added, "this will be the first time I've shared a bed with a female though... it should be interesting."

Ishandra chuckled. "I think it's going to be an interesting night all around. I'm happy that I get to see it all too."

"Awww, you're blushing again, hon" Anubis said as he turned his attention back to Thomas. "That's so cute."

Thomas felt his face heating up at both of their words, but he also felt a warm glow from Anubis' attentions. He looked back at the jackal's face as Anubis gazed upon him. Those yellow eyes stared straight into his. He leaned forward until their lips touched again. He closed his eyes as their mouths came

Will A. Sanborn

together. Their kiss was tentative at first, but he felt Anubis' mouth opening to him, gently urging him on. He gave a deep sigh as he responded.

Kissing the jackal still felt a little awkward, but he slowly got the feel of Anubis' muzzle against his. Like with Ishandra, it was a variation on a theme, and he experimented in his actions to find what worked best between them. He could feel the warmth between them spreading as they worked at the kiss and his own arousal was growing stronger. He was giving in and responding to the moment, even if it did seem a little strange to find himself kissing a guy. It felt oddly enjoyable as well. He felt his arms clutch at the jackal's back, pulling them closer together as their kiss deepened. He pressed his body against Anubis and felt the jackal respond in turn.

He felt Anubis' tongue against his. It was larger than Ishandra's and thinner than a human's. It was longer than Thomas', and while less supple than the dragoness', it was still more flexible than his own. The feeling was awkward for a few moments, as he got used to the new sensations. He tried his best to play along. He opened his mouth a little wider and brushed his tongue against the Anubis'. The jackal responded by pressing against him and Thomas let out a little whimper. Anubis gave a moan of his own as Thomas pushed back against him, moving their bodies closer together. Thomas felt the wonderful ache of arousal as his hips met the jackal's.

Thomas reveled in the warmth between them as they continued to kiss and grope one another. His mind soon focused only on the pleasure and arousal he felt, not the different situation he was in. Anubis was another lover, a warm body of a friend to be enjoyed. With his mind preoccupied, the nervousness had evaporated. His hands came down to the small of Anubis' back and he squeezed him tight again. The jackal's body felt different than Ishandra and his other female lovers, but it also felt nice as he held him close.

Eventually they eased off on their affections. They had one last lingering touch of their lips before Anubis pulled his head back to look at him. Thomas smiled back at his jackal lover, his eyes sparkling.

"You're a nice kisser," Anubis said, and licked Thomas' cheek gently to add to the compliment.

"Thanks, you're pretty hot yourself" Thomas replied as his hand brushed past the jackal's tail to squeeze his butt. A brief complaint rose up from a distant part of his mind at that action, but he did his best to ignore it.

Anubis returned his smile, with his mouth opened partway to show his teeth. His ears twitched again as well. The jackal's yellow eyes regarded Thomas and gazed at him intently. Then Anubis reached out to take hold of Thomas' shirt. He pulled at it and finished the job of untucking it from Thomas' pants, then slid it up. Thomas heard a protracted breath escape his mouth as the jackal lifted his shirt up, exposing his belly and then his chest. He lifted his arms and surrendered to Anubis, letting him strip the garment from him.

With the shirt removed, Anubis brought his hands over Thomas' bare skin. "So lovely," he whispered as his fingers traced along Thomas' neck. Thomas let out another sigh, which spurred the jackal on. With slow persistence his touch slid down over Thomas' chest, then to his belly. Thomas wanted to submit to the pleasure, but as Anubis explored his naked torso, he felt his inhibitions returning.

Anubis' hand sank lower to hover over Thomas' crotch. He gave him a gentle squeeze through his remaining clothes, and Thomas let out another moan in spite of himself. He spoke out when the jackal made to undo the button of his pants.

"Wait" he said, his voice barely above a whisper.

Anubis regarded him with curiosity, then concern. "Is it going too fast?"

Thomas nodded.

"Would you like to have Ishandra help out?"

Thomas glanced over to her, to see the dragoness looking on with rapt attention and warm affection. He turned his gaze back to Anubis and nodded again. "Yeah," he answered. His voice came out a little louder that time. It felt both awkward and exciting to have her watching on, but the excitement was starting to win out.

Anubis' smile returned and Thomas noticed that his tail gave a slight twitch. The jackal took his hand and led him the few steps over to the bed where they joined Ishandra. The room came with a queen-sized bed, so there was plenty of room for all three of them. Ishandra had her back propped up on some pillows and she welcomed Thomas with open arms. He leaned back against her, sitting between her legs. Her skin felt good against his. Her arms came up to hold him and she gave his chest a gentle caress.

Anubis kneeled in front of him, off to one side. "There," he said, "Ishandra's going to help you get relaxed. We're both going to work on you and show you a good time." He paused then added, "but you don't have to do anything you're not comfortable with, hon. If you want I can just watch the two of you..." Anubis was only partly successful in hiding his disappointment at that thought, but his concern showed through as well.

Thomas shook his head. "No, I want to be with you, I just need to take it slow."

The jackal nodded and his expression brightened. His hand reached out to join Ishandra's in touching Thomas. Thomas let out another sigh, and then pulled Anubis down towards him. Their mouths met again in a soft kiss. He could feel Anubis' warmth above him and Ishandra's loving presence behind him. Her hands continued to caress him as he and the jackal kissed. He closed his eyes again and let himself get lost in the moment.

When they eased off from the kiss that time, Anubis seemed convinced once again of how wiling Thomas was. "So now what would you like to do?" he asked as he looked down at the lovely human laying beneath him.

Thomas mulled things over, and then replied "why don't we get you undressed?" Anubis nodded in affirmation. He guided Thomas' hands to his shirt and then joined him in tugging at it. Anubis helped him lift his shirt up, revealing the black fur of the jackal's belly. When Thomas couldn't lift his arms any higher, Anubis continued the motion, pulling the shirt up over his head and off his arms.

Thomas' hands came to rest on the space between the jackal's chest and belly. His touch was tentative at first, but then became bolder as he traced random patterns through the jackal's fur. "Your fur is so soft" he said as he looked up at Anubis.

"Thank you," the jackal let out with a sigh. "It feels good. I haven't had a human touch me in so long..." His words trailed off and the jackal's ears lowered, as he realized his poor choice of words.

Thomas stroked the jackal's side with a gentle, reassuring touch. "I understand, you find us as exotic as we do you..." He paused, and then added "I never thought I'd be in a situation like this, but I want to be with you, Anubis."

Anubis beamed down at him, and took Thomas' hand in his own and squeezed it affectionately. He then led Thomas's fingers to the button of his pants. He looked down at Thomas, his eyes questioning him.

"You do it," Thomas whispered. Anubis nodded and slowly worked the button free of its hole. Thomas felt Ishandra's hands touching him, giving him encouragement. His hands joined the jackals in pulling his pants down, to uncover his undies. Anubis wore a pair of bikini-cut briefs; their light blue color added a contrast to the jackal's soft black fur. His tail was twitching again, showing his excitement, as they slid the pants down off of him. There was a more obvious display of his arousal though. Thomas looked at the evident bulge in Anubis' briefs. The outline of jackal's erection was visible through the thin fabric as it strained against it, and it was impossible to mistake his intentions.

"Wow" Thomas whispered as his he slid his hand up Anubis' leg, drawing near the briefs. He traced his fingers along their contours and then rested his hand over the hard bulge in the jackal's undies. He felt the slight reaction as Anubis' cock twitched in response to his touch. The jackal let out a soft sigh as well.

Anubis' hand came to join Thomas' and rested beside it. The jackal looked down at him and smiled. "These can stay on awhile" he said, indicating his briefs with his finger. "I want to give my attention to you first."

The jackal's hands then came to Thomas' pants and this time he offered no resistance as Anubis toyed with the button holding them closed. Those fingers released the button, and then moved to slide the zipper down with slow precision. Thomas lifted his hips in response to Anubis' gentle pat on his butt and then the jackal pulled his pants off with quick enthusiasm. The garment was tossed to join the others lying strewn on the floor, leaving Thomas clad only in his gray briefs.

Anubis slid his hands up Thomas legs. "You look so sexy like that hon" he said. "And so eager too" he added as his hands traced over the outline of Thomas' erection through the cotton of his briefs. The jackal felt Thomas' cock react to his touch, twitching upward to meet the gentle pressure of his fingers.

Thomas also felt Ishandra's hands still holding and touching him. He let out a sigh from their combined attentions. He then heard her voice in his ear. "You do look yummy like that, hon." She focused her attention on Anubis and added "and you look hot yourself, lovely jackal. I hope I'll be able to see more of you later."

Anubis smiled at her, but his ears moved up and down in a quick nervous motion. "In due time, pretty dragon, but for now I think we need to see more of Thomas first." Anubis' smile widened as he looked back down at Thomas. "Ishandra is going to slip these off, then I'm going to get a good look at you" he said as his fingers continued to stroke him through the fabric of the briefs.

Thomas felt Ishandra's hands moving lower as she took the jackal's cue. Her fingers traced along the edge of his briefs, then slid under them. Anubis lifted his hand off of the bulge in Thomas' shorts to give Ishandra room to work. Her fingers gently pulled up on the cotton, lifting it from his skin. The head of his cock popped out and he sighed as he felt the fabric brush against it. He also couldn't help but look down and see her slowly revealing him to their eager eyes. He heard a soft chuckle coming from Ishandra and then she let his briefs fall back into place.

"Don't tease me too much" Anubis said as his hand stroked Thomas' belly, just below his navel.

Ishandra peeled back the cotton again, letting more of Thomas' erection escape. Thomas held his breath as she pulled his briefs down lower. It was so surreal to see Anubis looking down at him, the jackal's eyes showing his desire. At the same time Thomas felt his arousal growing as he was exposed to him. His cock twitched again in anticipation.

Once all of Thomas' privates were revealed, Anubis took the briefs from Ishandra's hands and finished the job of stripping him. He then turned his attention back to Thomas' crotch. His hands slid up Thomas' upper thighs, and at the jackal's gentle insistence, Thomas opened his legs wider to him. Thomas felt Anubis' hand reach up to cup his balls and he let out a moan as the jackal's fingers stroked him and touched off sparks of pleasure.

"Very good," the jackal whispered to him. "You like that don't you?"

"Yes," Thomas answered in a drawn-out breath. "It feels so nice, Anubis..."

Anubis gave him a gentle squeeze, using the slightest bit of pressure and Thomas felt another ripple of pleasure. "It's so exciting seeing you respond to me."

The jackal's hand moved lower to touch the skin under his balls and Thomas' response was just as appreciative. Thomas felt a finger begin a tentative exploration along the cleft between his buttocks and his nerves tingled at that surprising touch. Then he felt the jackal's touch brush against his anus. He let out a surprised and worried squeak at that intrusion, and Anubis quickly withdrew the probing finger.

"Okay hon, that's too much for now, but how about this?" the jackal asked as his touch focused on Thomas' cock. He traced a single finger along it, and supplied a gentle pressure as Thomas' erection twitched again. The whimper he heard Thomas let out was answer enough to his question.

Thomas looked down through half-closed eyes to see Anubis' black-furred hand sliding slowly over his cock. The tip was dripping pre-cum and soon the jackal had the length of his erection slick with his excitement. The added lubrication made it easy for Anubis' fingers to slide over his skin. He shivered as his cock danced at the jackal's delicate and playful touch. Then he felt the jackal's hand grasping him, squeezing with a firm insistence. He let out a protracted groan to reward the jackal's attentions.

Anubis was looking into his eyes again, his gaze locked with Thomas'. Thomas saw the spark of desire in those yellow eyes as the jackal's tongue slipped out to lick his thin lips. With another move of deliberate slowness, Anubis lowered his head to Thomas' crotch, keeping his eyes locked with Thomas' all throughout the motion. The jackal brought his nose just above Thomas's hard cock and sniffed at it, taking a deep breath into his lungs.

"May I?" Anubis asked, as his tongue stuck out further.

Thomas hesitated. It took him a moment to realize what the jackal was offering, and then he felt a twinge of uncertainty about what it implied. His desired quickly won out and he gave the jackal a nod. "Please..." he whispered.

The first touch of Anubis' tongue along the shaft of his cock sent new waves of sensation through him. He stiffened then relaxed his legs in reaction to the pleasure. Ishandra had returned to stroking her hands along his torso as well. He let out a wordless affirmation in response to their combined attentions, and he closed his eyes and surrendered himself to the two of them.

A few moments later he felt the jackal's muzzle slide over his cock. He let out another moan as the wet warmth of the jackal mouth surrounded him. He lay there and basked in the love that was being shown to him. With his eyes closed he thought he couldn't tell who was slowly sucking his cock. It could be Ishandra taking him in her expert mouth. No, it felt slightly different. For one thing the jackal's tongue wasn't the same. The differences were good though and he thought to open his eyes. He looked down and saw Anubis' head bobbing up and down over his crotch. Another thought slid up from the back of his mind. This was a guy showing him such wonderful attentions, and yet it felt so good. At the moment it felt so right. "Oh Anubis," he heard himself say, his words coming out with a sigh.

Thomas reached down to stroke the side of the jackal's head as he continued to suckle on him. His fingers idly traced through the soft black fur again and he stroked at one of the jackal's ears. Anubis redoubled his efforts and Thomas felt his pelvic muscles flex in response, almost involuntarily. He could feel the heat building within him once again. The tension was mounting. He brought his hips up to meet Anubis' mouth, pumping against the jackal's motions.

Ishandra's hands moved lower, to stroke his belly and then the top of his crotch. Then he felt Anubis' fingers return to his balls. The jackal squeezed them as he took Thomas all the way into his mouth again. Thomas groaned in a mix of pleasure and tension. The need was building within him. Anubis' fingers became gentler, tracing along the contours of Thomas' balls, finding just the right nerves to touch. Ishandra's fingers moved with an empath's skill. They slid down to join the jackal's, and together the two of them stroked him closer to the edge.

Anubis' mouth and tongue were insistent as he took Thomas in again and again. Thomas could feel every touch and sensation. He thrust his hips upwards as he started to feel another tickle deep within him, another promise of release. Then the fingers stroking him touched the right nerve. He felt the flicker of pleasure burst into a flame and his climax hit him. He shuddered at the sensation and felt his cock surge inside the jackal's mouth. He let out a groan mixed with his breath as his stomach muscles tensed. He looked down through blurred vision and saw Anubis swallowing all that he was giving him. The sight of it, along with the spasms of pleasure, elicited another moan from him.

Slowly the climax faded and the bursts of pleasure died down. He'd closed his eyes, but opened them again as he felt Anubis licking his cock once more. The slow strokes of the jackal's tongue plucked at his over-sensitive nerves. He whimpered as Anubis washed the last remnants of his spent love from his flesh. When the jackal lifted his head to look at him, he flashed Thomas a smile as his tongue licked the outside of his muzzle. Thomas felt both the warmth of the afterglow and the growing feelings for his friend. He guided the jackal's head up to his and gave him a soft kiss. He tasted a faint hit of his salty presence as their lips met, but he was used to that from past experience; Ishandra being the most recent example. He pulled Anubis close to him and felt the warmth of the jackal's body and his soft fur against his naked skin.

Their kiss played out then they slowly eased off, after enjoying one another. Anubis regarded him and smiled. "So, you can have fun with a male and not feel bad about it, right?"

The answer was most definitely yes, but all Thomas felt he needed to do was return the jackals smile and give him an enthusiastic nod. "We still need to do something about you though..." he said a moment later, as he winked at Anubis.

Thomas' hand slid down the jackal's side to rest on his belly. Anubis' cock had gone down to semi-erect, but it was beginning to stir to life once again. There was also a small patch of moisture on the front of the jackal's blue briefs. Thomas' smile widened when he saw that and he continued to caress Anubis.

"You don't have to do anything," Anubis said. His was voice earnest.

"I know, but I want to." Thomas replied. "Besides, both Ishandra and I would like to see what you've got hidden there." He heard the dragoness give an affirmative sound from behind him.

His hands reached to grasp the jackal's underwear, and without much ceremony he slid the briefs down off the jackal's crotch. Anubis' cock sprang forth to their gaze. He was beautiful kneeling there with his undies pulled down to his knees. The skin of his cock was dark, almost matching the shade of his black fur, and his erection was standing at full attention. It was Thomas' turn to

Will A. Sanborn

explore his new lover and he returned the favor as his fingers reached out to stroke along the contour of the jackal's balls. The soft fur felt wonderful against his fingertips, almost like velvet. It was exciting to be touching another male. He heard Anubis sigh at his touch, and that too spurred him on.

"You look so beautiful," he whispered. As he gazed upon the jackal and saw him shivering at his touch, the image of an obsidian statue come to life drifted through his mind. Here was his own living god to worship.

"Come, lean back against me" he offered. Anubis was all too eager to obey. He turned around and slid his underwear the rest of the way off his legs, and then leaned his back against Thomas.

"That feels so nice," Thomas added as he felt the softness of the jackal's fur against him once more, now covering most of his body. He could also feel the heat of both of his lovers' bodies as he was sandwiched between them.

"Now we're going to see if we can get you off, lover" He whispered in Anubis' ear. "Ishandra is going to touch you as well." He spoke the last part loud enough for her to hear it. Anubis let out a whimper, but he could not tell if it was from his hand trailing down the jackal's body, or from the idea that a woman would be giving him pleasure. A moment later the dragoness' hands found their way to the jackal's body as well.

Ishandra started stroking along his neck as Thomas' hand reached the jackal's crotch. Anubis opened his legs to his touch and Thomas slid his fingers down to toy with the jackal's balls once again.

"That's it, just enjoy it" he whispered again. It felt good to be taking charge, now that he no longer felt awkward and was able to return the jackal's kindness.

His hand moved up slowly to take hold of Anubis' cock. He was reminded of how much it felt like stroking himself with the jackal in that position, except of course he couldn't feel the pleasure his touch was bringing. Anubis let out a soft moan which was enough feedback though. His fingers grasped the jackal's cock tighter, and they slid along the length of it. He soon felt the slick feel of skin against skin as his motions spread out the ample amount of the jackal's own pre-cum.

Another thought flashed up at him, this time another memory of him and his cousin playing together. He felt surprise at the warm glow it gave him. It didn't seem wrong now, the memory made him hot. He grasped Anubis' cock a little tighter as he thought back to that hot summer day in the barn, and their fumbling teenage experimentation. He heard the jackal sigh against his touch and he continued to stroke him.

His other hand slid down to give attention to the jackal's balls once more, his fingers caressing him through his fur. He could also see Ishandra's hands stroking Anubis' chest and belly. He closed his eyes and listened to the jackal's breathing as he continued to work him over. His hands slid up and down over Anubis' cock, squeezing and pumping him, urging him on to his own release. He got lost in it as the moments flowed into one another. He listened for Anubis' reactions as he varied his strokes occasionally, and tried to find the right touch to send him over the edge. Anubis let out another whimper as Thomas gave his hand a slight twist around the head of the jackal's cock. It was almost hypnotic hearing the jackal respond to his touches and he continued to toy with him.

And then suddenly her felt Anubis stiffen against him, and he heard a low groan escape the jackal's mouth. He opened his eyes and was rewarded with the sight of Anubis cock shooting white streams of cum across the black fur of his stomach. Thomas pumped him slowly as the jackal's climax died down, and he milked every last bit of pleasure from him. He felt the jackal shivering under his touches and he smiled. Finally he released his hold on him, and let Anubis rest in the afterglow.

"That was amazing" he whispered.

"Oh, thank you, hon" Anubis managed to reply.

Thomas held him and let him catch his breath some more. "Thank you, Anubis. This was special for me, more than I would've known."

"It was very special for me too, Thomas" the jackal answered, and Thomas hugged him.

"And thank you Ishandra," Thomas said, turning his head back as much as he could to address her. "It meant a lot to me, and it was special having you help us out."

"You're welcome hon," he heard her reply. "It was really hot watching the two of you and getting to participate in it."

He couldn't see her expression, but he guessed that she was smiling. He closed his eyes and drank in the presence of the two of them as they surrounded him. No matter how strange things were in the outside world, at that moment all that mattered was that he felt loved so very much.

◆ ◆ ◆

Thomas' dreams were more distinct that night. He found himself lying naked on a stone slab. It was cold against his flesh and he shivered as he lay there. The chamber he'd found himself in was only dimly lit from a couple of torches burning as they hung on the walls. His eyes slowly adjusted to the light, and then he saw two figures step out from the gloom. They were Anubis and Ishandra. He smiled up at them, but the looks they gave him chilled him. Their eyes fixed upon him with cold precision.

Anubis was dressed in Egyptian garb. He was stripped to the waist, save for a large piece of ornamental jewelry in blue and gold which covered his neck and upper chest. He wore a kilt-like garment covering his lower body and had thick blue and gold bands of metal on his arms, above his wrists. Ishandra was dressed in a robe of dark crimson.

He tried to move, to sit up and then realized that he was bound to the stone. Ropes held his wrists and ankles secure, and held him open to their scrutiny. He struggled against the bonds but they wouldn't give way. He saw the two of them looking at him but they showed no emotion in their eyes, not even dark amusement as he tried in vain to get free.

Anubis reached down to touch his chest, but the jackal's touch was methodical, not meant to bring any pleasure. "The sacrifice is ready" he said to Ishandra. She gave a silent nod and handed Anubis a silver knife. It caught a ray of light from one of the torches and reflected it for a brief instant as the jackal turned it over in his hands.

Thomas continued to struggle against the ropes, but they wouldn't give way. Then he tried to speak, to tell them who he was, to plead with them for his life, but his words would not come forth. He felt his throat constricting and then it was even hard for him to breathe. He gasped for breath and tried to speak again and the choking sensation only deepened. He saw Anubis holding the knife over him and he twisted against the bindings, shaking his head violently. Neither of them were concerned with him, nor did they pay him any more heed. Instead their eyes were focused on the knife which hung in the air above him. A second later Anubis brought it down into Thomas' chest with a swift blow. He felt the blade ripping into his flesh and felt the strangled scream trapped in his throat.

He came awake with a start, his body giving a quick jerk. He wasn't fully conscious and at first he didn't know where he was. Then he found himself in bed, spooned in between Ishandra and Anubis. For a second he wondered if he had actually screamed, but neither of his bedmates had stirred, so his reaction hadn't awoken them. He shivered as the dream came back to him. He could see Anubis plunging the knife into him and the dull memory of the phantom pain lingered with him. He let out a soft whimper and clutched at Ishandra for comfort. He felt Anubis move and he worried that he'd woken him. The jackal just snuggled against him in his sleep and then was still again. Thomas shivered at his touch, and then realized the specter from his dream was not the warm body pressing against his. He focused his thoughts on the warmth of his two lovers, and after awhile his tired mind found sleep once again. He was lucky and was spared any further possible torment from bad dreams for the rest of the night.

Will A. Sanborn

Chapter 11: St. Pauli Girl

Now spin that wheel, there's nothing to lose
Spin that wheel, it's waiting for you
Now spin that wheel, let the wheel decide
Spin that wheel, go along for the ride
    Devo, "Spin the Wheel"

The wheel is turning and you can't slow down
You can't let go and you can't hold on
You can't go back and you can't stand still
If the thunder don't get you, then the lightning will
    The Grateful Dead, "The Wheel"

Thomas awoke to Ishandra stirring beside him. The terror of the previous night forgotten, he sighed as the two of them snuggled. He cuddled against her and let himself slowly become more alert. Anubis appeared to be a heaver sleeper and did not wake. Thomas could feel the jackal's warm body against his back as focused his attention on the dragoness to his other side. He closed his eyes and wanted to rest there for ever. Eventually Ishandra's gentle affections become more-insistent nudges.

"Let's stay here a little longer," he whispered.

"We need to get up, it's going to be a busy day," she countered.

Finally she urged him up with the offer of sharing the shower and Thomas begrudgingly got out of bed. They headed for the bathroom and left Anubis peacefully sleeping away in the bed.

The warm water felt good, as did having an extra set of hands to help him get clean. "Last night was good" Ishandra commented as she was soaping him up. He nodded and she smiled at him. "See, you were able to share love with another man and it didn't kill you."

Her eyes were bright and happy as she offered that thought, but her choice of words jostled something in his mind. Suddenly the memory of his nightmare returned to him, and Thomas' face paled as the haunting images jumped out at him. He felt his body shake as he relived the scene of Anubis cutting into him.

Ishandra's smile evaporated. "Thomas, what's wrong?" she asked, her expression now showing shocked concern.

"I had a nightmare last night, a really bad one." He told her the details of the terrible dream. He watched her reaction as he described how the two of them had sacrificed him in some dark ritual. Her expression darkened as he finished.

Ishandra held him; her touch offered some amount of comfort. "That sounds terrible hon" she said as her eyes looked at him with deep concern. "I don't think you're feeling guilty from being with Anubis. You seem okay with that. It could've just been some wild random thought" she offered.

"Could it have been a premonition? Could being around you guys and all this growing magic have affected me that way?"

"Perhaps," she answered as she appeared to be mulling over that possibility. "I can't tell if you have any latent gifts for that or not... Death in those dreams is not always literal too, it could mean change, like in the tarot."

"It felt so real though, even though I know you guys would never do anything like that to me." He paused, and then added "normally I'd try to just forget a bad dream, but with everything that's going on, I don't know what to think of it... Do you know any more about what we're heading into?"

"No, I was going to try a divination this morning. I'll do that and focus the question on what might happen to you."

He hugged her. "That would help me feel better. Thanks."

When they were dressed, she left for Thoth's room to ask him if she could use it as a quiet spot for the divination ritual. Anubis woke up as she was leaving. Thomas saw the jackal stir and walked over to the bed. He sat down next to Anubis and placed his hand on the jackal's chest; he stroked him idly through the sheets.

"Good morning," he said as he looked down at Anubis. Even with the uncertainty about everything, and the lingering uneasiness from the horrible dream, he still good at seeing the jackal looking up at him.

"Mmmm," Anubis let out a tired sigh and smiled up at him. "Where'd Ishandra go?" he asked after a few seconds.

"She wants to try a divination to see if she can find out more information about what's going on."

"That sounds like a good idea."

Thomas hesitated, then added "I had a bad dream last night. With all the uncertainty, it really shook me up, so she's going to try and see if we're in any danger."

"What kind of dream?"

"Somebody killed me. I got stabbed with a knife." Thomas didn't offer any more details and Anubis didn't ask him to elaborate. He was relieved at that. He didn't want to see the jackal's hurt reaction if he told Anubis that he was the one that had sliced him open.

They stayed like that for a few minutes before Anubis sat up. Thomas hugged him and they shared a warm kiss before he headed to the shower. It was nice feeling closer to Anubis, and it helped take his mind of other things.

Ishandra returned about three quarters of an hour later. By that time Anubis had showered, blow-dried his fur and gotten dressed; he was sitting on the bed and waiting with Thomas. Thomas gave her a worried but hopeful look as she entered the room. "Did you have any luck?" he asked her.

"A little," she replied. She looked both concerned and a little discouraged. "I was able to get a slightly better sense of things, but it's still very cloudy. I still can't get a good idea of what it is we're going to find."

"So you don't know what we're up against?" His voice resonated his worries.

"I'm sorry, hon. As I said, divination is tricky under the best of situations, and it looks like what we've got here is something unusual."

"Did you talk with Thoth about it?" Anubis asked.

"Yes, he and I both can't get a strong grasp on it, but it's definitely something to do with a good deal of magic, which could tricky, and dangerous." She paused, then looked at Thomas, and continued. "Thomas, I was able to get a sense of how it might affect you though, and that worries me."

Thomas didn't like the sound of that, but all he did was stare at her, as he waited for her to elaborate.

"With the dream you told me about, I wanted to make sure that it wasn't a chance of a premonition. It doesn't look like you'll be killed, but you could be hurt, maybe hurt pretty bad." She paused again, and as she looked at him, her eyes showed more of her concern and devotion. "I did get a very strong feeling that whatever it is, it is going to involve a major change, something that will impact your life."

"So it's like you said, the death in the dream could mean change?"

"Yes, hon, but I couldn't get a clear idea of what the change is. That worries me."

"So now what do we do?" Thomas asked her. His face was starting to pale again. He felt Anubis' hand on his shoulder, steadying him, offering comfort, which he willingly accepted.

Ishandra took one of his hands as well, as she sat there in front of him. "Now it's up to you, Thomas. You need to decide if you want to continue along with us or not."

"How can I do that? We still don't know enough about it make an informed decision."

"We know that there's a possibility that you could get hurt, and I don't want that."

"Neither do I," Anubis said, as he squeezed Thomas' shoulder.

"But wasn't there always a chance of that?" Thomas asked; his voice was beginning to sound agitated. "I mean we started out on this with the angel telling Mark that we could be dealing with the end of the world, so I think we always thought it could be dangerous. Plus, it sounded like you guys needed my help, for whatever reason."

"That is true," Ishandra replied. It sounded as if she was making an effort to keep her voice calm.

"I feel like I've been through so much already, and now you're saying I should just walk away from it? I don't think I could do that... I guess I want to see where this ends up."

"So you want to continue, are you sure?" Ishandra focused her gaze on him; she studied him with her eyes.

"I'm still not really sure about anything on this strange quest, but I want to stay and help if I can. I'll continue to follow you." Thomas' voice shook a little as he finished. Even as he said he felt unsure, but the feeling of commitment pulled at him as well.

"You're very brave, hon" Ishandra replied, as she gave his had a reassuring squeeze.

"I wish I felt that more" Thomas answered.

"You will, when you need to. You've shown a lot of potential already, and I know you have more."

"Yes," Anubis agreed, as he spoke in Thomas' ear. "You've proven a lot already."

As they packed up and got ready to head back out on the road, Thomas hoped they were right. He still didn't feel all that brave, but he hoped he could gain strength from his friends. He tried not to think too much about the unknown, or what Ishandra had said. It didn't sound like they had much chance of knowing or changing the future. Now that'd he'd decided to follow them, he was committed to whatever lay ahead, and dwelling on it didn't seem to do much good. Of course trying not to think about it was a lot easier said than done.

◆ ◆ ◆

They were on the road again after breakfast, just like they'd done the last several days. They didn't have far to travel that morning though. Thoth could feel whatever it is they were tracking getting closer all the time. They were able to narrow it down to one of the twin cities early on, heading into St. Paul instead of Minneapolis. Then it became a task of trying to zero in on the mysterious source of energy. That wasn't particularly easy though. Thoth could sense rough directions and changes in the intensity, but it was by no means a precise measurement. They drove through the city, slowly spiraling closer to the target or at least that's what they hoped. In the end, it didn't seem like they could narrow it down any closer than a general area a few miles wide. By that point it was getting on into the afternoon and they need a break, so they stopped for a late lunch before they risked starting to get discourage.

They found a small diner that looked like it would serve decent food. The place wasn't too crowded when they came in, since it was past the lunchtime rush. Their waitress, Debbie, was a statuesque blond of Teutonic beauty. She spoke with a lingering hint of a Scandinavian accent and seemed a little out of place serving tables in the small restaurant. She was quite pleasant and hardly even batted an eye at their motley crew. Then again, it was a big city, so there were a good number of exotics around.

Will A. Sanborn

The food was not only decent, but the kitchen was efficient too. Their meals came up soon after they'd ordered. They discussed their situation while they were eating.

"So now what do we do?" Thomas asked Mark.

"I'm not sure, Thomas" the older man said as he turned his attention towards the ibis. "Thoth, do you have any idea how we can get closer?"

Thoth shook his head. "Unfortunately at this point it feels like the energy is all around us. I can't get a good bearing on it."

"If Thoth can't get a good reading and Ishandra's divinations don't help, that doesn't leave us with much, does it?" Thomas asked. His voice had the barest hint of defeat to it. He paused, thinking for a couple of moments, then added "Mark is it possible to get a hold of the angel and ask her for assistance? Could you pray and ask her to appear?"

"I've been praying, but it doesn't quite work that way, son. The heavenly agents don't just show up at your beck and call. They do things on their own time, when the time is right. I have been praying for guidance and I believe that somehow we'll find what we're looking for."

Thomas' expression was dubious. "I guess so," he managed to reply.

"You've got to be patient, hon" Ishandra said as she gave him a reassuring look. It didn't help him feel all that much better though. "Perhaps Mark is right and that it isn't time yet. Perhaps you need to be ready for it, or we all need to be ready."

"I don't know how much more ready I can get, especially given that we still don't know what it is we're facing. All we know is that it's some strange magical force and it sounds like it's potentially very dangerous. How do you prepare for that?"

"Whatever it is, you know we'll do our best to protect you..." Anubis started to say.

Thomas' attention was distracted from him for a second though. From his vantage point he saw their waitress, Debbie, staring at them from only a couple of tables away. From the expression on her face, it looked as if she'd heard what they were saying. When she noticed him staring at her, her expression turned from worried interest to a mix of surprise and anger.

Thomas continued to stare at her, feeling shocked himself. The next thing he knew he saw her turn around and she started walking away briskly. Thomas managed to nudge Anubis, and point in her general direction. It was a few seconds before he could articulate what he wanted to show his friends. By the time he was able to blurt out "she heard us... she's getting away," Debbie had reached the entrance of the diner. Just as Thomas got his companions to look in that direction, she was dashing out the door.

Mark was the first one to react. He was up in a snap and ran out the door to chase after her. He came back inside a couple of minutes later, shaking his head. Instead of returning to the table though, he rang the bell on the counter. The rest of them looked on and watched as the manager came out. They couldn't hear what the two men were saying; they were too far away for that. The manager looked confused at first, then a little put off. He disappeared out back for a few minutes while Mark waited, and when he returned his expression was a little darker.

Mark continued to discuss things with him, and they could see he was working on his persuasion. His expression remained stoic, but there was a restrained intensity showing through as well. Finally they saw the manager point to a coat rack behind the counter and single out one of the coats upon it. When Mark gestured toward the coat, the manager shook his head, but after a little more of Mark's quiet persuasion, he relented and handed the garment over to him. They saw Mark give the coat a quick inspection, as he looked through the pockets. He then appeared to have found something, because his expression lightened. He gave the manager a small smile and then returned to the table. They saw the manager looking back at him; he shook his head as Mark walked away. He looked relieved, but still wary, and he soon returned back into the safety kitchen.

Mark's smile increased as he sat back down at the table. "What was that all about?" Anubis asked.

"Well, I chased after our waitress, but I couldn't find her. She had too good of a lead on me and got out of sight too quickly. She must know something to have taken off like that though, so I figured she'd be a good lead."

"That makes sense, but what happened with you and the boss?"

"Oh, I just told him that our waitress had run off for no good reason. He couldn't understand why she'd leave, but after checking out back and in the restroom she was nowhere to be found. I told him I was worried about her and that being a believer, I wanted to see if there was anything I could do to help. Maybe she needed to hear the word of God."

"You actually said that?" Thomas asked, shaking his head slightly.

"Yup," Mark continued as gave an enthusiastic nod to Thomas. "It's a stretch, but it does have a grain of truth to it. Besides, it sounded better than telling him about the threat we're trying to track down. People tend to be more receptive to ministry."

"And you know how persuasive he can be when he wants to," Ishandra said as she flashed a smile. Thomas nodded; he'd seen some of that for sure.

"So when he said that she'd left her coat, I got him to let me look through it. Then I found this." He held out a simple calling card which read 'Sons of Canute lodge' and listed an address. "I asked him where this was and he said it's only a few blocks from here. I think we should check it out."

The others all nodded. "It does sound like a possible lead," Thoth agreed.

"I can't believe it" Thomas said, shaking his head.

Mark smiled at him again. "He does work in mysterious ways sometimes."

Thomas had little to counter that with, but it probably didn't matter. They'd be following that lead no matter what. He shrugged and joined the others as they finished their lunch. It would at least give them something to do.

Will A. Sanborn

Chapter 12: Norse Meets West

We come from the land of the ice and snow
From the midnight sun where the hot springs blow
How soft your fields so green, can whisper tales of gore
Of how we calmed the tides of war, we are your overlords
On we sweep with threshing oar, our only goal will be the western shore
    Led Zeppelin, "Immigrant Song"

They finished eating quickly. They agreed that it was best not to give the manager too much time to reconsider letting Mark have the address he'd found in Debbie's coat. They doubted the man would do anything. They hadn't done anything wrong, so he couldn't call the authorities or anything, but it was best not to stick around and risk any trouble. Besides, they had a lead that needed to be explored.

It didn't take them too long to locate the Sons of Canute lodge. Even though they didn't know the area, they only had to drive around for about ten minutes before they found the right street, and then the address itself. The lodge was a small, ordinary building. It looked like just about any other social club, which they assumed the organization was. Either that or it was a religious organization, but the building didn't resemble a church or temple of any sort.

The door was unlocked and they entered the building. They walked into the lodge to find the main room, which looked like a meeting area. There were stacks of folding chairs leaning against the walls and a small podium. There was a folding table and an American flag at the further end of the room. Save for those furnishings, the room was empty and nobody was around. It felt odd to have walked in an unlocked door to find the place deserted.

There was a door on the side wall, but when they checked it out, it only turned out to be the bathroom, which was also empty. There was a hallway off the main room which led to a set of stairs going up to the second floor. There was a door on the far wall as well. Mark wanted to check that out first, before going upstairs, so they moved towards it to investigate further. They were all walking cautiously, even Mark. The door opened to reveal the kitchen, which didn't appear to hold anything of interest, until Thomas noticed the door at the far end of the room.

There was a lock on the door, a dead-bolt, which seemed out of place and at odds with the rest of the building. They were on the right side of the lock though, the one which could be opened with out a key. The door looked to be made of very heavy wood as well. Mark opened the door slowly and they saw a flight of steps leading down into the basement. Mark flipped the switch near the door and a light came on below them, illuminating the way.

They went down in single file, first Mark, then Ishandra, Thomas, Thoth and Anubis. At the bottom of the flight of stairs, they found themselves in the musty cellar. The floor was poured concrete, but the walls were made of the old stone foundation. The stones cemented together gave the place a rustic look. The cool stone room was lit with a single 60-watt bulb and there were no windows, so it wasn't too bright. It was bright enough to see around the room, but it felt gloomy.

There wasn't much in the basement, just the oil furnace, stacks of boxes and some other detritus. Then Thomas saw it, the stone table at the other end of the room. It was made of a slab of rock, set on top of columns of cinder blocks. The construction wasn't elegant, but it appeared to be very sturdy. It seemed out of place down there, as if it'd been built for a specific task. Thomas took one look at it and the memories from the nightmare came flooding back over him.

He stopped cold. "That table, it's like the one from my dream..." he said.

Ishandra turned and looked at him. "The altar?" she asked him.

He nodded, as he continued to stare at it. His face went pale as those terrible images flashed in his mind's eye all over again. "It's like the one I was tied to. It looks like it's meant for a sacrifice."

"Indeed it was fashioned for that purpose" a voice behind them spoke out. They all turned to see a man walking down the stairs. His skin was pale but his hair, which was wild and unkempt, was a brilliant red. Behind him came three other men.

The pale man with the fiery hair grinned at them as he reached the bottom of the stairs to face them. "Yes, a sacrifice has been planned, and it looks like you may have provided for it." Mark stepped forward when he heard that. The man continued to grin at them as he looked the members of the group over. "Hmmm, it seems that we may have some of the old ones here," he said as he glanced at Ishandra, Anubis and Thoth. "But I would imagine that you have mortals in your group as well" he continued as he turned to face Mark and Thomas.

"Thomas, get behind us" Ishandra said. Her voice sounded urgent.

Thomas heeded Ishandra's warning and backed up. At the same time Mark pulled out his knife and took another step towards the red-haired man. "Very well, I did expect some sort of a fight," the pale man said. "This should be interesting." As he spoke he revealed a knife of his own.

The other three men with him brandished similar weapons as well. Ishandra, Anubis and Thoth moved forward to hold them off, but when the red-haired man saw they didn't have any weapons, he looked even more pleased with the situation. "Don't worry boys," he said as he addressed his followers, "they may be immortals, but they're no stronger than you are. Use the blades to slow them down, and I'll take care of the humans."

Thomas backed up further when he heard that. A chill ran through him at the realization that he was the only member of the group who could be seriously hurt. He felt so helpless as he watched it, but there was nothing he could do; self-preservation overshadowed the terror and shame he felt at not

Will A. Sanborn

being able to help his friends. He saw Mark step up to confront the pale man with the fiery hair, while the others each squared off against one of the other men.

Mark was doing the best of the group. He managed to block every move the red-haired man threw at him, and he dodged the blows of his foe's knife with ease. The others were doing okay, but were not as adept at fighting as Mark was. Thomas saw Ishandra throw a punch at the man she was facing, and he recoiled from the blow. The next moment he saw Thoth take a knife across his chest. The quick slice ripped open his shirt and blood started oozing out. Even though he knew the wound wouldn't be permanent, Thomas still recoiled from the sight. Anubis made a grab for the knife his attacker was wielding, but that only gained him a savage cut across his hand.

Mark went on the offensive, and made a couple of swipes at the red-haired man. His opponent laughed at him as he deftly dodged the blade. Then the man hesitated in his evasive movements. It was only for a second, but it gave Mark the chance to connect with him. In a flash Mark's blade made contact, slicing the man's pale skin and spilling blood. At the same instant, the man's ploy became apparent. With his hesitation and by allowing Mark to cut him had also allowed him an opening. Even as Mark's knife was cutting him, the red-haired man reacted. His own knife swung forward and stabbed into Mark's stomach. Thomas let out an audible gasp. History was repeating itself.

"Not so tough are we now?" the red-haired man laughed at Mark. "This game is a little different." He withdrew his knife and grinned at the sight of Mark's blood as it spilled out of the fresh wound. He laughed again as Mark let out a low groan.

Mark gritted his teeth and shook his head as he stared his opponent down. "It may be a little different for you too" he managed to say through his pain. He grimaced and jabbed his knife at the man again. His move caught the red-haired man off guard and he got another slice cut into him. It wasn't a very deep one, but it proved the point.

"Very good" the man chuckled as he dodged Mark's next blow. "I see you're very determined. That will make things more entertaining."

Mark continued to fight him, but it quickly became a stale mate. Both men avoided the other's blows and neither opponent was able to score any more damage against the other. The other members of the party were faring slightly worse. Since they weren't armed, they were getting worn out by their attackers; it was a slow but steady downhill progression. They could fend them off well, but the blades were able to connect with them occasionally, opening up new wounds which would take time to heal. The pain was still real though, and each cut took away from their concentration.

The cuts on the red-haired man's chest were drying up as he continued to spar with Mark. Then he noticed that Mark's wound was also closing up, and for the first time his face showed genuine surprise. "Well, this is very interesting indeed. I didn't peg you for an immortal as well. Tell me, what god are you?"

"I'm not a god, but I serve Him" Mark spat back.

"And what about your friend?" the man asked as he gestured toward Thomas? Mark didn't reply, but his defensive reaction was enough of an answer. The look of shock on Thomas' face gave further proof. "Very good, we still have a sacrifice left after all."

Mark pushed against the red-haired man; his resolved deepened at the man's threats. Thomas started to move sideways, as he tried to make his way towards the stairway. There was nothing he could do to help his friends, but at least he could save himself. With him gone, they wouldn't need to worry about him either. He felt a pang of regret stab at him as he thought that, but he focused he thoughts on getting out of there. Mark saw what he was doing and he started maneuvering his opponent, and slowly turned him away from Thomas.

It seemed to be working. Thomas inched his way along the wall, as he kept his eyes on all of their adversaries. His friends were keeping them busy, so he was able to move closer to the stairs. He backed up slowly, watching the melee and making sure no one was moving towards him. He was nearing the front of the room and the safety of the stairway when he felt something behind him. An instant later a pair of arms reached forward, grabbing him in a strong grasp. One of those hands held a knife which pressed against his neck, quelling any thoughts of resistance within him.

"Alright, nobody move or the kid gets it" he heard a woman's voice yell. A second later they all turned to look in his direction; their expressions quickly turned from shock to horror. Thomas couldn't see who held him captive, but the rest of the party had a good view of Debbie, the waitress from the diner, as she held Thomas with a knife to his throat.

"Drop your knife" the red-haired man ordered Mark. When Mark hesitated, he added "do it or we'll see just how mortal your friend is." Mark glared at him, but let the knife fall from his hand.

"Take hold of our friends," the man then commanded his followers. "If they give you any trouble, we kill the kid." The three other men moved behind the three gods. They grabbed their hands behind their backs and held them tight. Thomas felt the dull ache in his stomach as he saw his friends forced into surrender. Even from several feet away he could read their expressions and see the anger and fear on their faces. The man holding Ishandra gave her a rough squeeze. Her nostrils flared and she tensed, but she didn't fight it.

"You stay where you are," the red-haired man said to Mark, and then he walked towards Thomas and Debbie.

"It looks like this is going to turn out better than we'd planned," he said as he studied Thomas. With him so close, Thomas could see that the man's eyes were green, not a cool green like Ishandra's, but a brighter shade. They felt fiery and piercing in their brilliance as the man stared at him. The pale man reached down and grabbed Thomas' hand. He grinned at Thomas' shock when he brought his knife close to the young man's flesh. Thomas tried to pull back, but he felt Debbie press the cold steel of the knife against his neck. It was just the slightest bit of pressure, but it got her point across. He forced his hand to go slack and closed his eyes. A second later he felt the sting as the knife sliced into the flesh of his palm. He heard the man laughing and he forced himself to open his eyes.

The red-haired man watched him bleed. Thomas gritted his teeth and tried to take deep breaths as he fought against the pain. He turned his eyes away from the ragged cut on his palm and the blood spilling out of it. Instead he forced himself to look up at the man who was tormenting him. The man paid him little heed at the moment though; instead he was intent on watching Thomas' wound. After a few minutes, when the flow of blood didn't dry up and Thomas' flesh didn't stitch itself back together, the man nodded and smiled.

"Very good, it appears you are mortal after all." He turned his gaze to address Debbie as she held Thomas. "Thanks to you warning us about this group, Rahe, we not only were able to get the jump on them, but we have our sacrifice now as well. You won't need to find someone for that anymore." Thomas felt his body shudder at the man's words. He also saw his friends react and struggle briefly against their captors, but they didn't fight too hard for fear of Thomas' immediate safety.

The red-haired man turned away back to address the other member's of the party then. "Well, since you've gone to the trouble of meeting me, I suppose introductions are in order. My name is Loki and these are my followers." He then gestured back towards Debbie. "This lovely woman is Rahe, a valkyrie who has joined me to savor the coming chaos. I doubt any of you know who I am, but that is irrelevant, for my time will soon come regardless of whom remembers me."

"You remind me of Set" Thoth spat out. "You look as hideous as him and are probably just as crazy."

Loki just grinned at the Egyptian. "I do not know of the god you speak of. Our dynasties were far apart, and I imagine we both come from worlds whose glory has faded. That doesn't matter now though. The other gods had me imprisoned for centuries, but as time passed and they lost followers, their powers faded. Mine did as well, but it also meant that the spell binding me was weakened and I was eventually able to escape after long having been in captivity."

"I couldn't return to Valhalla, so I headed to this new land, where some of the descendants of our original followers had settled. I knew I'd be far away from the other gods and free to enjoy my freedom." He paused, and then continued. "Freedom without the powers I'd enjoyed before grows tiring though. I've gotten bored with this world and living in exile. Eventually I settled on waiting for the final battle which will end the world. After years of study, I've found how I can bring about Ragnarok."

"But why would you want to end the world?" Ishandra asked as she regarded him with a cold gaze.

"Once this world is destroyed, a new one will rise from the floods that cover the remains of the old one. The current age will be over and a new one will begin. I intend to take advantage of that and claim power while things are fresh. I will be a proper god once again."

"But how do you know you'll survive to make it to the next world?"

"A rare astronomical event is about to occur. Tonight key heavenly bodies are going into an alignment that happens only once a millennium. By performing a sacrifice during that alignment, I will call forth the powers to upset the balance of this world. I and those who follow me will be protected by the release of the powers, so we can watch in the destruction of this world. The Fenris Wolf will be released to swallow the sun and the moon, throwing the world into darkness. Monsters long fettered will be freed to fight against those whom imprisoned them, and the battle of Ragnarok will begin. It will be glorious chaos. I cannot wait to see those gods who opposed me finally destroyed."

He grinned once more and pointed towards Thomas. "Thanks to you, we now have our sacrifice. I can think of one who's not more fitting than a member of a party who came here to try and stop me. I don't know how you fell in with these immortals kid, but you're going to regret it." Thomas felt his stomach clench even tighter. He saw Mark step forward, but Loki just shook his head at him.

"Don't even think about it. I can just as easily kill your friend right now and Rahe can find another one to replace him. She can find some lonely man at the dining place to seduce to following her back her. All you'd accomplish is having your friend die sooner, and without any purpose. Let him be the one to usher in the destruction of this world. Like me you no longer have any ties to this world, so just let it go."

Mark scowled at him, but made no further motions. Loki nodded and grinned back at him. Thomas then heard Rahe whisper in his ear. "I'm going to have fun with you. Your death with be sweet to savor, the first of many. Loki has promised me the great carnage."

Loki turned and smiled at her. "Yes that is true, my love. The battles will be magnificent visions to behold."

He then addressed the group one last time. "It was lucky you came upon us today, for the alignment occurs tonight. I will return then to carry out the sacrifice." He paused, and then added. "Do not think of opposing me, we will be even better armed when we return, and if you chose to let your friend die prematurely, we will have another mortal waiting ready. If need be, one of my followers will lay down his life for me."

The men following his orders didn't react to his last statement. Their faces stayed cold and determined as they held onto their prisoners. Thomas' friends only looked on with their faces masks of contempt and hatred, but they didn't make any moves. Loki ordered his men to release Ishandra, Thoth and Anubis one by one, and had each of the gods back up against the wall. He ordered

Mark to do the same. Loki's henchmen then walked past him, Rahe and Thomas to go up the stairs.

Loki followed them, with Rahe bringing up the lead. She held tight onto Thomas all the way up the stairs, and only released him when they'd reached the door. She let him go and pushed him down in a quick motion. Thomas stumbled, and almost fell down the stairs, but managed to grab a hold of one of the rocks in the wall to break his fall. It was enough of a diversion to allow Rahe to slam the door behind her though. A second later they heard the dead bolt click into place as the door was locked. Then the lights went out and they were all plunged into darkness.

Will A. Sanborn

Chapter 13: A Glimmer of Hope, a Shadow of Doubt

Water's flowing though my veins
Nothing ever stays the same
Water's flowing down my side
Turn the water into wine

Where's the courage I once had?
Where's the strength I once possessed?
To stand up tall and face the music
Laughing in the face of death

Here's a boy whose hands are bleeding
Though he's never had a scratch
Glory come and glory be
Water's flowing now at last
    Oingo Boingo, "Glory Be"

Ishandra's voice came up from the darkness. "Thomas, are you okay?"

"I guess so," Thomas managed to reply. He groaned as he tried to stand up and then winced as the pain shot through his hand again. He was still shivering from the aftermath of their encounter with Loki and Rahe.

A second later a dim light lit up the darkness of the cellar below. He made his way down the stairs to see Mark had produced a flashlight. Its light gave enough illumination for him to make out his friends as they stood there looking at him. Mark bent down to pick up his knife, which he'd dropped earlier. Loki hadn't bothered to grab it, but then again it wouldn't make much of a difference.

Ishandra walked forward to meet him. "I'm so glad you're okay, hon" she said in a low voice. Thomas only nodded. He was okay for the moment, but that didn't offer him much solace.

"Oh, your hand "Ishandra added as she saw and remembered the wound Loki had given him.

"Use this," Mark said as he handed her a handkerchief. Ishandra made quick work of tying it around Thomas' hand. He winced again as she bandaged him up, but said nothing. Ishandra then gave him a quick hug for support. Anubis and Thoth stood nearby to offer their wordless support as well.

"I'm sorry I got you into this Thomas," Mark said after a long silence. Thomas glanced at him and the man's eyes were lowered, his gaze not meeting Thomas'

"I made the choice to come, and again this morning I made the choice to stay with it..." His voiced didn't end up sounding as convincing as he'd hoped it would.

"Still, I wish I hadn't dragged you into this, son. I never thought anything like this would happen."

"You did say it could be dangerous," Thomas offered, but his voice still sounded flat. He paused, and then felt the reserves of his strength falling out from him. "I don't want it to end like this" he said, and he heard his voice beginning to crack.

He felt both Ishandra's and Anubis' reaffirming touches, which helped stabilize him a little. Mark stayed silent. Thomas continued. "It doesn't make sense, to come all this way, just to die..."

Mark shook his head. "No, it doesn't," he agreed and his voice sounded low as well.

"But why even have me along, if I'm the only one who can be killed?" Thomas asked, his voice growing bitter. "We fell right into the trap of what we're trying to stop..."

"We can't always hope to understand the plans" Mark offered, but even he didn't sound convinced.

"Well I don't like it." Thomas spat out. "It's so unfair..."

A feminine voice interrupted him. "I know it's unfair, Thomas, and for that I apologize."

They all turned to see a woman standing behind them. She was wearing a white robe which seemed to give off a soft glow. Thomas blinked and as he stared at her he could make out the forms of wings behind her, sticking out from the back of her robe. She gave him a tiny but genuine smile, and her warm eyes looked upon him; they showed sincerity and care. She had a simple and honest beauty about her.

"Hello Thomas," she said. He felt a warmth within him as she spoke. "I know this is difficult for you, but please believe me when I saw that we did not have you come through the journey just to die in vain. Things can still be saved. You were chosen because we believed you could handle the task set before you."

Thomas blinked at her. "So you're saying I'm some sort of a Chosen One?"

She gave him another warm smile. "In a way, but not the way you're thinking of. You're not the only person who could undertake this task, but you were one of the better candidates who were near to Mark and Ishandra, so we made sure you met up with them."

"So this whole trip and everything was set up? It was all planned out in advance and none of it was real?"

She shook her head. "No, we can only make small things happen. He doesn't like to show his hand too greatly. We did give you a nudge or two in the beginning, to get you to meet up with Ishandra, but from there it's all been your doing. We cannot go against free will."

"So I could've walked away at any time?" Thomas asked, his voice still sounded incredulous.

Will A. Sanborn

"Yes, we were hoping that with your curiosity awakened, you'd decide to go along with them. We also hoped that Ishandra would have a positive effect on you with the relationship between you two. You've grown a lot from that. Anubis has helped as well."

Thomas felt his face heat up again, but she paid no attention to his blush and perhaps she didn't even see it in the low light.

"We hadn't planned on you two joining the group" she continued, as she looked over at Anubis and Thoth, "but you've both helped out so much already. When we saw you were investigating the disturbance as well, we nudged things a little more to have you all meet up. Thoth, your knowledge of magic will be of great use and you can help Ishandra." Thoth nodded at her, and looked on silent, as if he was waiting for her to continue.

Thomas wasn't as patient. "But what is this all about? Why am I here?"

"You were brought here to do what is required of you" she answered. Her face remained calm as his expression darkened. "You do not understand it now, but you will. Everything that has happened on your quest to get here will serve in that understanding. You have grown so much in dealing with everything you've been through. It has prepared you for what is to come next."

She continued as Thomas gave her a confused and aggravated stare. "I know you don't believe it, but you are ready to undertake the task. Have faith in yourself and trust your friends. I cannot tell you what is to happen, you must figure it out for yourself. I'm sorry for that, but we believe in you. I will tell you that you will not die tonight. You will be required to make a sacrifice, but it is not the one you think, and you will live through it."

"But..." Thomas started to speak, but she held her hand up to quiet him.

She then turned to face Thoth. She reached into her robe and retrieved a scroll. "Take this and you will know what needs to be done" she said as she handed it to him. "Both you and Ishandra will understand."

She turned to Mark who met her gaze. "Mark, you've done very well in this task, you all have. It is almost finished, but you will all need to help Thomas. Continue to care for him as you have been." Mark gave her a solemn nod, but there was a glimmer in his eyes.

She finally returned her attention back to Thomas. She put her hand up to his face to touch his cheek, and he felt her calming presence wash over him. "We ask the most of you, Thomas. We're sorry for the troubles you've been through, and the trial still awaiting you. We wish you peace and strength. We thank you for your sacrifice and know that you will be okay."

Before Thomas could manage to say anything, she turned and walked away from all of them. She moved towards the wall of the cellar and then passed through it, as her body dissipated like a vapor. As she vanished, the heavenly glow around her faded too, and they were left with only the dim light from Mark's flashlight once again.

Thomas felt his body tremble. "I don't understand" he said as he shook his head slowly.

"You will, son" he heard Mark say.

Thomas looked at him. "How do you know that? For someone who came to help, she didn't do all that much."

Mark gave him a solemn nod. "I know, Thomas, but that's how she can be sometimes. Mysterious ways and all that. They like to work with a light touch. Remember she didn't tell me the whole story about myself until she thought I was ready for it." He paused and fixed his eyes intently on Thomas. "I know it isn't much consolation, but if she says you'll make it through this, then you will."

"You're right, it doesn't help that much" Thomas replied. His words sounded hollow and he heard the bitterness in his voice.

Mark reached out to place his hand on Thomas' shoulder. "Try and have faith, son. God's grace is with you." Thomas offered no reply to that and after a few moments, Mark withdrew his touch. "I am sorry we got you into this, Thomas, but we'll get you through it."

"Thoth, let's have a look at that scroll" Ishandra spoke out to cut the silence. Thoth nodded and the two of them started opening what looked like an ancient piece of parchment. It crinkled as they unrolled it, but it stayed intact.

Thomas felt his legs starting to get tired, so he sat down. Anubis sat down as well and motioned for Thomas to sit with him. Thomas took the jackal up on his wordless offer and joined him as he sat against the wall. He leaned against Anubis for support and rested his back against him. Soon he felt the jackal's arms coming around him and he let himself fall into Anubis' embrace. He closed his eyes and let himself go numb for, as he tried to block out the rest of the world.

Some time later he became aware of Ishandra and Thoth talking. He opened his eyes to see the two of them musing over the scroll. They were sitting down as well, and from his vantage point he could see part of the writing on it. Whatever the text was, it looked like it belonged to a language that had probably died a long time ago. It didn't look like it was written in Egyptian hieroglyphics. The characters looked like scrawls of wavy lines, but they appeared to be more like letters than pictograms. They had a slight resemblance to Celtic runes he'd once seen, but even then the similarity was fleeting. Whatever it was, he couldn't make any sense of it.

"Can you guys actually read that?" He asked them, as his curiosity overshadowed his doubts and fears, at least for the moment.

"A little bit" Ishandra replied as she looked up at him and showed him a slight smile. "Thoth is having better luck than I am, he's picking it up quicker."

"My connection to the magic is helping me with it," Thoth added as he gave Thomas a nod. "The magic of the scroll is helping me to understand this language. It was slow to start, but we're making progress."

The two of them turned back to their work. They poured over the foreign symbols on the page, and talked amongst themselves. Thomas looked over at Mark and he was sitting there with a look of concentration on his face. His eyes were closed and he looked to be either meditating or praying, or both. Thomas leaned against Anubis and tried to relax. The jackal's warm presence did offer some comfort, but his mind felt numb.

Things continued that way for close to a couple of hours. Thomas tried his best to rest and had some margin of success with that. He knew it wouldn't help him to panic, but he couldn't stop worrying. Mark continued to pray, and Thoth and Ishandra continued to discuss the scrolls. Then after a long time, he heard Thoth's voice rise above the low murmur.

"Yes, that's what she was talking about. That's how it'll work..." Thomas looked over at the ibis, to see him pointing to a section of the ancient text. "You see these glyphs here, they turn the magic back in on itself and combine with this part here, and then the protection will be complete." Ishandra studied the scroll for a few seconds, and then nodded her head. Thomas could see a smile creeping across her snout.

"What did you find?" he asked them. His voice betrayed the flash of hope he felt.

"I believe we've discovered the secret of these texts," Thoth answered. He sounded the most excited that Thomas had ever heard him.

Thomas felt Anubis give him a reassuring squeeze and he looked over to see that Mark had opened his eyes and was watching Thoth and Ishandra intently.

Thoth continued. "We've figured out what the scroll is all about. It describes the ceremony that Loki is planning to do. It details the sacrifice and how the spell will offset the balance of things, releasing chaos. The magic it will generate is impressive." He paused, and then added "we've found a way to counteract the spell."

"What do you mean?" Thomas asked. His voice was hushed.

"There is a spell we can use which will reverse the flow of magic and turn it back in on itself. Instead of flowing outward, it will be reflected back on you, the sacrifice. All that magic can be focused to save you. Instead of dying, you'll live, and you'll be healed."

"Do you really mean it? Are you sure?"

Ishandra nodded, and her smile grew a little wider. "I've been looking over Thoth's shoulders and I can read the runes almost as well as he can now. From what I see, it looks very promising. I have faith that it will work."

Thomas felt a shiver of excitement run through him, but then his thoughts cooled. "So they'll still try to sacrifice me? They're still going to cut me open?" He felt his gut clench at the thought, and again the visions and the phantom pain from his nightmare came back over him.

Thoth nodded his head slowly. "Yes, I'm afraid you'll still have to endure that, Thomas. I believe that's what the angel was talking about. It will be a lot to go through, but we will be here with you, and you can make it through it." Ishandra's smile faded, but she continued to look at him, and he could feel the emotion in those soft green eyes. He also felt Anubis hugging him in support.

"So I'll survive, I will be healed?"

"Yes, Thomas" Thoth replied again.

"So what do we have to do?"

"We need to transfer the spell onto you, so it will be there to protect you" Thoth answered as he and Ishandra scooted closer to Thomas. He came to sit in front of Thomas and Ishandra was off to his side.

"Can I please use your knife, Mark" Thoth then said as he turned his attention to the older man.

Mark didn't move and his eyes narrowed on the ibis. Thomas saw Ishandra's expression darken as well. "What do you need the knife for?" Thomas heard himself ask. His voice cracked as he spoke the words.

Thoth's reply sounded very cool and controlled. "The glyphs of the spell need to be transferred onto your body Thomas. They must be made permanent so there is no chance of them being erased during the sacrifice. If that were to happen and the spell was incomplete, you would die, and this world will end..."

Thomas shook his head. "No, please tell me you don't need to do this."

"I think he's right, hon" he heard Ishandra say and then felt her touch on his arm. "We need to make sure the spell is perfect and that you will be safe."

"But if you cut all these spells into me, then how are you going to keep Loki from noticing that?" Thomas asked. His voice was sounding as desperate as he felt as he struggled to defeat their logic. "If he suspects we're trying something, then he'll just sacrifice someone else and we'll have failed."

Thoth nodded again and winked his eye. "I can mask the spell, so that once it's complete, only the ones who wrote it, and of course you, will be able to detect it. To anyone else your flesh will appear unmarred, even though the cuts will be there." He paused, and then added "I know this is a lot to ask of you, Thomas. It is more than you ever could've dreamed when you agreed to join us on this quest, but it is the only way. Please trust me."

Thoth then turned back to Mark. "Can I please use your knife? Please trust me that I would not cause him any more harm than in necessary."

Mark was doing his best, but his sadness showed through his stoic expression. He eyed Thoth and hesitated for several seconds, then reached down to hand him his knife. After the ibis had the tool, Mark turned to face Thomas. "I'm sorry son" was all he said.

Thomas felt Thoth's avian eyes looking at him again. "Please take off your shirt" the ibis said. His voice was low and it sounded restrained.

Thomas delayed responding for as long as he could, but after several seconds he finally obeyed. His arms felt numb as he slowly lifted his shirt up. When he got it up to his head, he felt Anubis helping along with it.

Thoth reached out his hand to trace a single finger along Thomas' chest. Thomas heard his breath escape him as the ibis touched his skin. "I am sorry I have to do this Thomas, but it's the only way." Thoth's eyes looked a little softer as he looked at Thomas and continued to speak. "I don't want to have to hurt you, but I want to see you protected... I will not cut deep, just enough to get through the skin."

Will A. Sanborn

Thoth paused, and then added "there will be some blood. Anubis, we'll need your shirt to clot the wounds once I've made the marks." Thomas felt the jackal shifting behind him and he moved his back forward to allow Anubis to remove his own shirt. His body felt numb and heavy as he went through the motions, complying with Thoth's orders.

Anubis brought his shirt down to rest on Thomas' lap. Thomas felt Anubis hugging him again and dimly registered the feel of the jackal's fur against his back. Thomas felt Thoth's touch on his belly. "I'm going to start down here and work upwards, it will be easier to deal with the blood that way."

"How many symbols do you need to make?" Thomas asked as he saw Thoth unsheathe the knife and get ready to use it. He couldn't help but look at the blade as it approached him.

"Several, it will take some time. I'll try and make it go as quickly as possible, but I need to make the glyphs very carefully... You don't need to watch, Thomas. Try and relax."

"I'm here for you, hon" he heard Anubis whisper in his ear, and he felt the jackal's hand on his chest.

Thomas forced himself to close his eyes and he tried to lean back as far as he could against Anubis. The muscles in his back were tight though and he couldn't stop tensing them. He heard Thoth ask Ishandra to hold the scroll open for him, and then a few seconds later he felt the knife against his skin. There was a brief instant where it was just pressing against it and he could feel the cold steel pricking his skin, sending an itching sensation through him. He felt his stomach tense up, then the blade cut into him and he felt the savage, burning pain. He cried out, and his scream cut through the silence of the room. He felt Anubis' other hand plaster itself against his mouth, as the jackal tried to stifle his outburst.

The blade withdrew from him, and the pain reduced in intensity, though it still stung at him. "Here, take this." He heard Thoth say. A second later he realized the ibis as addressing him as he felt something brushing against his cheek. He opened his eyes to see Thoth holding the leather holder from Mark's knife. "Bite down on this, it will help some" Thoth said. Thomas felt a brief flash of humiliation wash over him, but he complied and opened his mouth.

Anubis took the bundle of leather and slipped it into Thomas' mouth with great care. Thomas bit down upon it and gagged at the taste. He forced himself to nod to Thoth though and then closed his eyes. He tried to prepare for the next attack, but it wasn't much use. The next slice of the blade was just as painful. He clenched his teeth down on the leather and the only help it gave was to choke back his screams. Thoth made another cut and then another and he felt the pain burn through him.

He heard himself whimper as Thoth continued to work the knife on him. His body tensed up again and he felt the muscles of his arms and legs tighten in response to the attack on his flesh.

"You're doing well," Anubis whispered in his ear as he held Thomas. Then another flash of pain seared through him.

Thoth was methodical in his work as he carved him up. Thomas heard his breathing loud in his ears as the air rushed through his nostrils. Each slice of the knife interrupted his labored breath as he choked back his cries. He then felt Anubis' hand bringing the fabric of the jackal's shirt against his tortured skin. The pressure made his wounds cry out again, and it blended in with the fresh pain Thoth continued to wreak on him.

Thomas felt himself twitching against the jackal and the ibis' combined assault. He tensed his stomach muscles again in an effort to hold still. He felt his breath exhale as a low moan rumbled through his throat as Thoth made yet another fresh wound.

Slowly he succumbed to the pattern of the attacks. The pain wracked through his body, but he found if he concentrated on his breathing it helped. If he timed his breaths right, he could shift some of his focus away from the pain, and every little bit helped. He lost himself in the assault his two friends were forcing upon his body, and he only dimly registered the slow movement of the blade as it traversed up his torso. He listened to the regular bits of encouragement Anubis whispered to him, and forced his mind to focus on the jackal's voice, taking him a little further from the pain. Ishandra offered her own words of comfort as well, and he tried to let both of his friends' voices sooth him. The agony was still present, but it was dulled some. He lost himself in the moment as timed slipped away from him.

Some time later, he heard Ishandra tell Thoth to wait and the blade ceased cutting into his flesh. He opened his eyes to see what was happening and immediately regretted it. His vision was blurry, his eyes having filled with tears, but he could see enough. He couldn't help but to look down and he recoiled from the sight. The image of his skin covered in ragged wounds, forming strange characters cut into his flesh, as they all seeped blood, sent a terrible tremor through him. He saw the fabric of Anubis shirt was drenched in blood and stained a dark crimson too. He felt his body shake and saw Thoth pulled the knife back so he wouldn't accidentally cut him.

Thomas felt Anubis' hands holding him tighter and he forced himself to close his eyes once again. He turned his mind inward again and focused on the rhythmic sound of his breathing. Then he heard Ishandra speak.

"Thoth, take a look at these runes here, I think you may be mistaken." Thomas felt his body tense again, but kept his eyes closed.

"What do you mean, Ishandra?"

"Look here. I don't think that when the magic is focused back on Thomas, that he'll just be healed..."

Thomas felt the scroll move against his leg as Ishandra directed Thoth's attention to the section she was talking about. Then he heard Thoth exhale loudly. "Oh..."

"You see it too, don't you?"

"Yes, those glyphs could have a different meaning than what I first thought. You're thinking it's more than just the restoration of life, aren't you?"

Thomas opened his eyes again, but forced himself to look straight ahead and focus his attention on Thoth and Ishandra's faces. They both look perplexed. He shivered as new worries stole in upon him.

Ishandra gave a solemn nod. "I believe the healing is a lot more permanent."

Thoth studied the scroll for several minutes. Thomas could feel the tension as they waited for him to speak. His pain seemed a little further removed as he waited for the ibis to confirm and explain Ishandra's suspicions. He shifted his gaze to Ishandra and she gave him a worried expression. Then he glanced over to Mark to see the older man looking upon the rest of them with grave attention.

Finally Thoth looked up from the scroll and spoke. "Yes Ishandra, you're right, I'm sure of it." His gaze came to rest on Thomas and he continued. "Thomas, the spell will work and you will be saved, but there's more to the sacrifice that the angel spoke of than what we first thought."

Thomas felt his stomach tighten up and then let out another whimper as a fresh wave of pain rolled over him. He then spit out the bundle of leather between his teeth so he could speak. "What do you mean?"

"I mean that you will be healed, but as Ishandra said, the healing affect of all of that magic will stay with you. It will change you..." He hesitated, as if trying to find the right words. "In affect you will not be sacrificing your life, but instead you death."

Thomas stared at him through watery eyes; the understanding felt just out of reach of his grasp. Then he heard Mark speak. "You mean that his life will be saved just as mine was, don't you?" Thoth turned to face Mark and nodded.

Thomas felt the cold wave of realization grip him. "So I'll be immortal too, won't I?"

Again Thoth nodded. "This changes the nature of things, Thomas. You're being asked to take on a lot more than I originally told you... Are you willing to take on that change?" Thoth paused again. "The spell isn't completed. We can stop if you want..."

Thomas heard the heaviness to Thoth's voice, and he felt the weight of consequences crushing down upon him. What choice did he really have? It wasn't just the desire he felt to save himself, he felt the responsibility which had been thrust upon him. He shook his head. "No, we can't turn back now..." He felt as if he was being pushed until his back was against the wall, then there was only one way to go. He felt the helplessness flood down over him, and surrendered to the circumstances. "Continue with the spell" he whispered to Thoth.

He closed his eyes and felt Anubis guiding the piece of leather between his teeth again. He bit down on it and waited for the next cut to come. The fresh searing mark of pain helped to block out the thoughts which tore at him. Again he focused on his breathing and surrendered himself to the strokes of the knife.

◆ ◆ ◆

When it was finally over, he felt Thoth touch him gently on the shoulder. He opened his eyes slowly and remembered to look at his friend's face and not down at his tortured body. "It's finished." Thoth said. His voice was calm. "You did very well Thomas. You are very brave."

Thomas couldn't think of anything else to reply except "thank you," but that was sufficient. He heard Ishandra and Anubis offer similar words of comfort and praise. He glanced over at Mark and saw the older man regarding him solemnly. Mark then nodded and Thomas could see the emotion brimming in his eyes.

Ishandra moved closer to Thomas and reached out for him. It hurt him to move, but Thomas made the effort to crawl into her embrace. He let out another whimper as all the wounds complained at once. He was beyond caring and he just fell against her body. Anubis moved over as well to add his warmth to Ishandra's'. Thomas welcomed it and focused on their presence against him. He felt Ishandra as she brushed her hand through his hair with an idle motion and he closed his eyes again. His mind and body both felt numb and he gave in to the fatigue. For the moment he welcomed the escape his light slumber gave him.

Chapter 14: The Moment of Truth

Now darkness has a hunger that's insatiable
And lightness has a call that's hard to hear
I wrap my fear around me like a blanket
I sailed my ship of safety till I sank it
I'm crawling on your shores
    Indigo Girls, "Closer to Fine"

And from the wreckage I will arise
Cast the ashes back in their eyes
See the fire, I will defend
Just keep on burning right to the end
    Asia, "Sole Survivor"

Thomas felt Ishandra gently touching his shoulder as he lay against her. Anubis was leaning against him as well, adding his presence for support. Thomas slowly moved to sit up and he let out a groan as tiny explosions of pain radiated from his stomach and chest. Anubis' shirt was against him. The fabric irritated his wounds, but he kept the bloody rag there, as it covered them up.

"How are you doing, Thomas?" Ishandra asked him?

He turned slightly so he could see her face as she looked at him. "I don't know, Ishandra... as well as I can be, I guess." His voice belayed his weariness.

"You're doing well, hon. You're very brave." Her voice was soft, but strong.

He shook his head. "I don't feel very brave."

"But you are," Anubis added. "You've taken everything that's come up in stride."

"He's right" Ishandra agreed. "You've got a lot more strength than you want to believe in. I'm proud of how well you're pulling through this." She paused, and then added "you're going to get through this, no matter how hard it is."

Thomas felt himself shiver at her last comment. The realization of the impending sacrifice flashed up at him and he tried to push that thought out of his mind. He didn't want to imagine all that it might entail, and even the fleeting images which came to him were enough to send sharp chills through him.

"I feel like I'm just reacting to things though" he answered. "It's like I don't have any other choice." Neither Ishandra nor Anubis said anything, so he continued. "I decided to come along, without knowing what I was up against, and now I have no choice but to go through with it."

Thoth spoke up. "If I'd know about the full extent of the protection spell from the beginning, would you have decided not to use it?"

Thomas turned his head to look at the Ibis. Thoth's eyes met his. "That's a hell of a choice to make, either to be dead or be immortal" Thomas said. Thomas felt Anubis squeeze his hand as he spoke.

"If you had a choice to be able to walk away from the sacrifice, would you?" Thoth replied.

Thomas gave his head another small shake. "I don't know. I wasn't given that chance..."

"All that matters is that you're rising to the challenge, hon" he heard Ishandra say. "That says a lot about your strength of character."

"It's still not fair" Thomas heard himself answer. "I guess all of you know what that's like though" he added as he turned to look at Mark.

Mark gave him a slight nod. "I know it's hard to take in right now, son, and you've got a heavy burden to carry." He paused, then added "You may not believe it, but you'll come to deal with it all, in time."

Mark then concluded with "I also believe that we're never given anything that we don't have the strength to handle. We can't hope to understand God's plans, but He wouldn't have you suffer without a purpose and without the support of friends to help you through this."

"We'll be here for you, through it all" Ishandra agreed. On one hand that was a small consolation for what lay ahead of him, but he also felt the load on his heart lighten as she spoke it.

Thomas looked at Mark and he felt his eyes starting to water again. "Mark, would you pray for me?"

"I would be honored to do that, Thomas" Mark answered. He bowed his head and closed his eyes. Thomas saw Thoth doing the same; he glanced at Anubis and Ishandra and they were following suit as well. Thomas closed his eyes and joined them.

Mark began to speak; his voice was soft and earnest. "God, above us and all around us, please offer us peace. Thomas has a great trial approaching, one that is going to test all of us, but him especially. Please give him the strength to face it, the faith to get through it, and ease his suffering as much as possible. Please help all of us to understand Your will and help us carry it out..."

As Mark spoke, Thomas did his best to open himself to the older man's faith and tried to push his fears away from him. He felt a longing for that peace, but also for Mark's spiritual connection. If nothing else, he appreciated the sentiment at least, and he let his mind focus on that.

◆ ◆ ◆

Just before midnight the light came on. The light from the naked bulb lit the basement in a harsh white light, overpowering the faint light from Mark's flashlight. Thomas felt his body jerk in surprise and he saw them all jump a little at the sudden change. Mark and Thoth were the first to rise, they got up just as they all could hear the deadbolt unlock.

Thomas stood up and was supported by both Anubis and Ishandra on either side of him. He winced once again as the wounds on his abdomen cried out at the sudden movement.

"Take it easy hon, we're here for you" he heard Ishandra whisper in his ear. It didn't help take away the pain in the pit of his stomach which had been gnawing at him as they'd waited out the evening.

"Mark, hide this" she said as she grasped the shirt Thomas still held against his cut flesh. She pulled it out of his grasp and tossed it to Mark. The older man was quick to toss it in the corner, behind one of the boxes, where they wouldn't see the bloody rag.

Thomas yelped as the fabric rushed across his skin and assaulted his fresh wounds. "I'm sorry, hon" Ishandra whispered to him. "We can't let them know about the protection spell."

Thomas couldn't help it and he stole a look down at his chest and belly and recoiled at the bloody sight of his ripped skin. The ragged cuts forming the alien words made it almost look like it was someone else's body. The wounds had clotted up for the most part, but as he'd moved, they'd started to seep blood again.

"Won't they see it?" Thomas asked as he felt another tremor run through him.

"No, the spell will blind them to it, they won't even see the blood."

"It's true," Anubis agreed, "as soon as Thoth finished, it disappeared. You look normal, I can't see a thing." The jackal then added, "I'm so sorry you have to go through all of this, Thomas, you don't deserve it." Thomas felt Anubis' firm grip on his shoulder, steadying him.

"You'll get through this," Ishandra added. "We'll be here for you." At that point they heard footsteps coming down the stairs, so Ishandra whispered one more thing. "You can't let them know you've been marked with the spell. Don't let on that anything's different."

Thomas gave his head a slight nod. He could feel his stomach twisting tighter into knots, and now he had to worry about them touching his wounded flesh and acting like he wasn't injured. He closed his eyes and focused on the dull ache in the pit of his stomach, as he tried to pull his attention away from his burning skin.

He opened his eyes a few seconds later to see Loki, Rahe, and their followers reaching the bottom of the steps. Mark and Thoth had stepped in front to confront them and Mark had drawn his knife. Loki let out a laugh as he looked at Mark's solitary weapon.

"Oh please, you know you can't beat us" he challenged Mark, as his followers and Rahe all showed the knives they held. "We've won and we're going to have our sacrifice." Loki's eyes burned with cold fire as he spoke.

"We could make it difficult for you..." Mark countered.

Loki stepped closer to Mark. "It wouldn't matter. Even if you wasted your friend's death, we've got other willing subjects to take his place." He paused as he glared at Mark, and then added "and we could make your friend's death linger on. Rahe hasn't had a good kill for a long time and she'd love to savor this one..." Thomas saw the valkyrie flash him a ravenous grin and he shuddered once more.

Mark glared back at him and didn't move. Rahe and the three other men then moved forward. "Don't resist it" she said as she reached out to touch his arm and gave him a lascivious look. Mark swatted her hand away, but did not make any motions towards her with his knife.

"You're beaten," Loki said. "Let us have our sacrifice and we'll make it easy on him." Loki chuckled when he saw Rahe's look of disappointment. "I give you my word that we'll make it no longer than it needs to be."

He then looked at Rahe and added "You'll get your fun when the battle of Ragnarok begins. I don't care for one individual's suffering when the grand chaos awaits us."

Rahe nodded, apparently appeased. Mark cast a forlorn look back towards his friends and then let the knife drop from his hands. Thomas had a dull awareness of the ploy Mark was playing at, but the fear Thomas showed on his face was genuine.

Loki and Rahe both smiled at Mark's act of acquiescence and they stepped past him towards Thomas. "How touching, consoling the sacrifice" he said as he gestured towards Anubis and Ishandra both standing on either side of Thomas, holding him in a protective stance. "You've gotten him all ready too," he continued as he pointed to Thomas' bare chest. "Now, give him to me."

Anubis shook his head. "We'll take him there." Loki flashed him a cold look, and then gave an indifferent nod.

"Come on, you can do this" Anubis whispered as they started walking. Thomas' legs felt heavy and numb, but he managed to stagger along with the two of them holding him up. He felt his stomach twist again as he saw the stone altar in front of him.

Loki let them help Thomas up on the stone table, but his followers stood by, ready to take over if they needed to. Thomas felt the cold stone against the naked skin of his back and tensed up again. The cuts on his abdomen cried out and he did his best to stifle his whimper.

"We're staying here" Ishandra announced as Loki and his followers surrounded the table.

"Very well," the pale, red-haired god said. "I will grant you the privilege of watching the sacrifice to call forth the chaos. Don't try and interfere though, or I'll let Rahe have her fun with the boy." Thomas shivered again and looked away from Loki, turning his attention to Ishandra.

The three men took hold of his arms and legs in rough grips and held him down against the stone. Thomas closed his eyes and tried to squelch the fear he felt. "Very good" he heard Loki say.

He felt a hand touch him and his flesh cried out as those fingers traced over his chest. He felt his body jerk, but he couldn't move against the strong arms holding him down. He clenched his mouth and stifled his cry so it came out as a low moan. He heard a woman's laugh and he opened his eyes to see Rahe standing over him.

"Oh, so sensitive," she said as she leered down at him and give him another poke. His moan was a little louder that time.

"Rahe, you are bound by the oath I made," Loki said to her. His voice was cold and deliberate.

Rahe shook her head, but obeyed. "What a pity," she said as she withdrew her hand from Thomas. "I would've enjoyed playing with you, but there will be many others." Thomas' eyes followed her fingers and saw they were wetted with his blood. Neither she nor Loki noticed it though. Thomas skin still protested from her touch, even after she'd withdrawn. He took in several deep breaths, trying to dull the pain.

"It is time" Loki said. A moment later he started chanting. His voice was strong and commanding as he spoke in a foreign language. The incantation sounded old and ominous as he belted out the guttural syllables. Loki's voice grew louder as he continued the invocation.

Thomas looked up to see Rahe bringing her knife down towards him. He held his breath and waiting for the blow, but it didn't come. Instead she held the knife out in front of him; she kept it in his field of vision as she moved it back in forth in a fluid motion. Her hand danced with the blade in time with the Loki's syncopated chanting. She looked into Thomas' eyes and smiled as she caught the fear in them. She looked determined to get as much fun out of him as possible.

Thomas watched the blade as it swished back and forth and a new fear lashed out at him. What if Thoth was wrong? What if the spell didn't really work? He twisted against the strong arms holding him and let out another gasp as those bonds held fast. Rahe brought the knife in closer, then pulled it back in a quick swoosh.

She continued to toy with him, as she edged the blade closer and closer to his flesh. He felt himself try and inch away with each stroke, but he was unable to move. He felt the tip of the blade press against his neck, and then it was gone. The motion was like a quick breath of air against him, and he felt the stinging itch as his nerves burned from the pricking touch of the knife.

He whined again and couldn't help but look up at Rahe as she grinned down at him. She brought the blade in contact with him again, this time letting it linger there a little longer so he could feel the cold steel of it against him. She withdrew it with another deft motion and Thomas winced as he felt the blade bite into him.

She held the blade up in front of him once again, letting it dangle over his face, and then she brought it back down against his neck. Thomas tried to steel himself for another attack. He held his breath as he waited for another sting from the blade. Her motion was swift that time and she'd cut into him before he realized what was happening. An instant later he felt the blade slicing deep into his flesh.

He yelled out, his cries no longer restrained and his anguished voice sounded loud in his ears. The knife tore a searing swath of pain into his neck and he felt skin and sinew tear open. A moment later he felt a warm feeling rush over his cheek and shoulder. When Rahe withdrew the knife he then realized it was his own blood that he felt against his skin.

He shuddered as he saw the blood, his blood, dripping from the blade, and he turned his head away from it. His eyes landed on Ishandra as she stood beside the table watching the dark ceremony unfold. He tried his best to focus his vision on her face. She did not turn away from the gore and kept her eyes focused on him.

He heard Loki's chanting growing louder. He felt the hot pain as the wound in his neck poured out his blood. His mind was dulled, his worried thoughts replaced with a primal terror. He felt his heart beating harder and could sense his blood spilling out with each pump.

The light in the room seemed to dim as he felt himself growing weaker. Then a new sensation washed over him. He felt an itching in the wounds on his abdomen. As Loki continued to recite the words of the arcane spell, that itching became a burning. It started small and grew until his skin felt like it was on fire.

He let out another moan, but his voice was low and weak. Even as the pain continued to wash over him he had a dull awareness that he was fading. He was hardly even aware of the knife blade pressing against his chest. It was only when Rahe hammered it down in that he felt it.

The pain was a sharp spike that stood out against all of the other suffering. It tore into him with a white heat burning away everything else. He jerked his body again, but his tremor was weak. It was one last feeble attempt, then his body relaxed, ready to die. He heard his strangled scream and felt the fading tremors of his heart as it began to give out. His vision went dark and his mind embraced the oncoming oblivion.

Then the pain was gone; it was replaced with a warmth that washed over him. The warmth grew and threatened to burn him, but as it radiated through his body his nerves gave into the heat and ceased their protests. The heat felt white hot, like a fire surrounding him, but it washed away the pain and all he felt was the heat.

He opened his eyes to see the wounds on his stomach and chest were glowing. The blood lit up with a faint light that outlined the symbols of protection. Loki had stopped chanting and both he and Rahe were staring at the cuts covering Thomas' skin. From the looks of their faces the spell had finally been revealed to them.

Rahe gave the knife a twist in Thomas' chest, but it had no effect. Thomas didn't even feel the pain from it, just a dull, distant pressure. The energy outlining the runes continued to flicker and grew stronger. Thomas felt the heat within and surrounding him building hotter still as the magic symbols covering him grew brighter.

　　　　　　　　Will A. Sanborn

The lines of magic etched into his skin glowed with a white light that continued to pulse and grow brighter. The heat enveloped him in its embrace and he felt sparks of energy prickling his skin. The sparks grew in intensity. They itched at his nerves, but still he felt no pain.

The light from the symbols spread out. It flowed over his body like liquid flames. He could feel the energy growing in intensity as it became more visible. The magic washed over him, illuminating his skin. For a brief instant he almost thought that it looked like his flesh was melting or burning in the fire, but he was not afraid; a strange peacefulness had surrounded him in that glowing warmth.

The three men holding him down on the altar released their grasps on him as the energy spread the length of his body and licked at their hands. The two men holding his hands even backed up slightly as the light washed over him. The magic felt so warm now. He was surrounded by its radiance. The heat would've surely been unbearable if it wasn't for the magic protecting him. Instead he felt like he was aglow with the magic. He felt a strange calm was through him as he basked in the energy.

The magic looked even more like a fire that burned all over him, all through him, but left his body untouched. The flames grew wilder. They pulsated around him, and flickered with the growing energy. The itching sensation he'd felt increased, prickling at his nerves. It spread through him quickly, and it almost became painful with its intensity. Thomas wanted to scream from the stinging feel of it, but he couldn't make a sound, he couldn't even move.

The sensations ripped at his nerves, as the strange torture continued. Then, just as it threatened to become unbearable, he felt the tension reach a climax. There was a rush of energy all around him, and he felt it pop, spreading outward. The strange fire that lit around him flared up and exploded in a flash of light; then it died down and in an instant it was gone. All of the liquid light dissipated into the air and the energy had left him.

He felt he could move again and he slowly sat up. Loki and Rahe had backed up involuntary when the spell had reached its peak. Ishandra took advantage of the opening Loki left and reached out to help Thomas get up. He swung his legs over the side of the table and got up off the altar. His legs felt weak for the moment, but Ishandra steadied him. The two of them stepped back, away from Loki, out of his immediate reach.

The Norse god stared at Thomas for a moment, his face a mask of disbelief and growing anger. "What have you done?!" he spat out.

"We found a protection spell" Thoth answered. "As you can see it focused the magic back on the sacrifice. He's like all of us now and you can't touch him."

Thomas looked down and saw that the symbols of the protection spell were fading from his skin. Even as he looked the wounds were disappearing from his flesh. He felt a dull itch in his chest and then noticed the knife still sticking out from it. He gave it a distracted look, and then reached down to extract the blade from his body. There was no pain as he pulled the steel out, only relief as he scratched the itch. He stared at the knife in his hand for a second, and then tossed it to the ground.

Loki glared back at Thomas as he saw his mortal wounds disappear. "The portal you opened has been closed as well" Thoth added. "You'll get no more use out of it now..."

"No" Loki said as he shook his head. His eyes were wide and they burned with the intensity of his emotions. He stared at them for a few seconds more, and then he spoke again, his voice becoming louder. "No, I will not be denied!"

He turned in a quick fluid motion and was on the man nearest to him in a flash. He grabbed at him and pushed him down onto the table. Rahe reacted almost as quickly and she helped him hold the helpless man down. Loki brought his knife up to his follower's neck and sliced it open without any ceremony. They heard the man's scream gurgle as it stuck in his throat, and once again fresh blood came pouring out onto the stone table. The other two men came out of their stupor and rushed to obey their master. They held their fallen comrade down and grabbed at his limbs, holding him to the altar as his body thrashed beneath them.

Thomas saw it all, but it didn't register on him. The effects from the spell still lingered over him, and numbed him to the terror before them. He stood there in a fugue until he felt Ishandra pulling on him, nudging him to move. They backed away from the macabre scene and headed for the stairs at the front end of the cellar. They made their exit while their adversaries were busy attempting another sacrifice and slipped away without notice.

"See you in one thousand years" Thomas heard Anubis call back as they left the stairway and exited into the kitchen. It was doubtful that Loki heard him though, as he'd resumed his chanting once again. His voice was loud and there was a frantic element to it as well.

They had no trouble getting out of the lodge and made it to their car without incident. Thomas walked in a daze and only had a dull awareness of what was going on around him. He heard them praising his courage, but he could only manage the briefest of replies. It wasn't until they were in the car and Mark had taken them several miles down the road that the numbness started to leave him. He felt his body starting to shake as the numbness wore off, and the comfort Ishandra and Anubis tried to offer him was of little help.

Will A. Sanborn

Chapter 15: Aftermath

All the same, we take our chances
Laughed at by time, tricked by circumstances
Plus ca change, plus c'est la meme chose
The more things change, the more they stay the same
  Rush, "Circumstances"

Everybody's smoking and no one's getting high
Everybody's flying and never touch the sky
There's a UFO over New York and I ain't too surprised
Nobody told me there'd be days like these
Strange days indeed, most peculiar, mama
  John Lennon, "Nobody Told Me"

Thomas didn't stir when Ishandra left the bed, neither did he hear the shower running in the bathroom. When they'd arrived at the hotel late the night before, they'd helped him undress and get into bed, and then he'd passed into unconsciousness. He'd been worn out from stress and sleep had claimed his tired body and mind. The sleep had been deep, devoid of dreams. He'd been spared any more nocturnal assaults, having lived through a real enough traumas already.

Thomas hadn't heard Ishandra moving around the room and he only stirred when he felt the gentle presence of her sitting down on bed next to him. Even then he was slow to stir from slumber. He didn't come fully awake, but he opened his eyes enough to squint at her as she sat beside him.

She reached her hand down to rest on his chest through the sheets. She kept it there and regarded him with a warm look that showed some concern hidden beneath it. After a few moments that concern faded slightly and a smile crossed her muzzle.

"Good-morning hon, how are you feeling?" she asked him. Her voice was low and soft, so as not to wake Anubis, who was still asleep.

Thomas blinked at her. His mind was still sluggish and he searched for an answer. "Okay, I guess" he finally replied after a few moments.

She nodded. "You had a hard night, but I can tell you're doing better now." She paused, then added "I'm sorry to wake you, I just wanted to make sure you were okay, hon. You can go back to sleep if you'd like."

He nodded and let his eyes close. A second later he managed to open them again. She bent her head down and let her lips touch his. It was a soft kiss, gentle and reassuring. He responded in turn and closed his eyes once more.

"You get some more rest then hon" he heard her whisper in his ear. "I'm going to leave you guys alone and let the front desk know we'll be staying past check-out, that way there's no rush."

He nodded but he kept his eyes closed. He could feel the want for sleep stealing over him and he didn't fight it. Her hand brushed across his chest, giving him a gentle touch through the sheets once more. Then he felt her weight shift and she got off from the bed. He heard her walking and then the door opened and closed, but he only focused on the warm feeling he felt lingering over him. He rolled over and found Anubis' body under the covers and pressed against the jackal's warmth. He then surrendered to sleep once more.

◆ ◆ ◆

He came awake the second time much more slowly. He gradually became aware of the warm body against his and then realized it was Anubis he was pressed against. He heard himself give a soft sigh as he snuggled against the fur of his back. He was so soft and warm and Thomas felt safe and secure as he lay there against his jackal lover.

The minutes passed and as Thomas became more awake he eventually felt Anubis stirring against him. Anubis woke up just as slowly as Thomas. The jackal stretched and out gave his own little contended sigh as he pressed his body back against Thomas. They lay there and cuddled, their hands touching each other with slow, idle movements.

Thomas let himself get lost in the moment, but eventually it was time to get up. It was he who finally made the decision and got the two of them out of bed. When they entered the bathroom he caught sight of himself in the mirror and quickly turned away. He was a mess and his hair was tangled and matted. It was much worse than a simple case of bed-head; it was clotted with clumps of something he could guess at but didn't want to think of. He had a flash of memory from the events of the evening before and he tried to force the image from his mind.

It wasn't much use though. When they were under the warm water of the shower and Thomas was trying to relax, he opened his eyes and saw the dark crimson stain running down his front. He looked down and saw it was forming a small puddle at his feet, to slowly be swallowed up by the drain. He realized it was coming from his hair as the clotted mess was loosed up by the water pouring down on it. He couldn't fight the realization any longer. It was blood, or remnants of it. It was his own blood, which had been spilled from the sacrifice the night before. The hot water was dissolving the dried gore, making it liquid again and it was flowing from him. He was reminded of how his blood had poured fourth while he lay on the stone table and he felt a shiver run through him.

He closed his eyes, as he tried to shut out the view, and then another shudder came over him. He'd been like that since last night. He'd slept like that and what's more, Ishandra and Anubis had slept beside him while he was tainted like that. He felt unclean and ashamed at the thought. Why hadn't they cleaned him up before? Why had they left him like that?

Will A. Sanborn

He felt Anubis' fingers going through his hair and he gave a soft whimper. He kept his eyes closed.

"Shhh, hon" he heard the jackal whisper. "It's not that bad and we'll get you cleaned up quickly. It'll be okay."

He tried to relax as he felt Anubis' hands moving the soap over his head. He was mortified at the state he was in, but he was getting clean. He remembered how he'd been the night before. Even after calming down from the aftermath of their escape from Loki and Rahe and their followers, he'd still been pretty stressed. When they'd found the hotel he was ready to collapse, so his friends and lovers had saved him any more trouble and had just let him sleep.

He sighed as he felt the gentle touch of the jackal working his fingers through his hair and over his scalp. It would be okay. It would all wash off. He would have no scars and there'd be no more blood, so he could try and forget it. He felt the tingle as another shiver ran down his spine. He knew that forgetting it wasn't going to be that easy though. Getting rid of the physical evidence would be much easier than those lingering memories. He let out another whimper and tried to think of something else.

"There, all done" he heard Anubis say.

He opened his eyes and blinked at the water streaming down over his face. He looked down and saw his chest and belly were clean. He cast a wary glance down further and saw that his feet were now only standing in clear water. He looked back up at Anubis and cast a smile at the jackal. He didn't have to work at the smile. Seeing that he was clean lifted his spirits and he felt a small feeling of relief wash over him, along with the warmth of the spray of the shower.

Anubis returned his smile as the jackal stood there looking back at him and holding the soap. Thomas threw his arms around him and pulled the jackal in close. "Thank you," he whispered as he felt Anubis' body against his.

The jackal responded in turn and held him in a warm, tight hug. "You're welcome" he gave a simple reply to Thomas. "You're going to be okay, hon."

Time stood still between them as they embraced under the warm shower. Thomas leaned his head against Anubis and closed his eyes. He then felt the jackal's hands moving slowly down his back, sliding the soap along his skin as they did so. Thomas let out a small sigh and gave Anubis a squeeze.

The jackal's hands moved slower down his back. When they came to his buttocks, Thomas felt the soap glide over them. His skin tingled as Anubis moved his fingers across it with gentle movements. The jackal's touch slowly became more suggestive. Thomas felt Anubis rubbing along his hip, washing the area in slow, circular motions.

The jackal's hands then moved back to tease along the cleft of Thomas butt cheeks. Thomas felt another shiver run through him, but this one was welcomed. Anubis was gentle in his explorations this time and Thomas did not resist the jackal's advances. He felt the soap slide down between his cheeks to his inner thighs. His body stiffened as he felt the jackal's tender touch. He gave out a moan and felt Anubis continue his efforts.

A small thought in the back of his mind was illuminated briefly. It was different to be with Anubis without Ishandra. Perhaps it still felt a little odd, but it also felt right. He ignored any remnants of doubt. He gave into the moment and felt his concerns melting from him as he was surrounded by the warmth. Thomas tightened the embrace on his lover, and took in the comfort that he offered. He felt his arousal growing as Anubis worked him over and he grasped at the lovely jackal's back, and pulled him in even closer.

◆ ◆ ◆

Thomas had been quiet through most of breakfast. He'd enjoyed the company of his friends; being with them helped him feel better, but his mind was still sorting through things. There hadn't been much conversation in general, as they'd sensed his mood and let him have some peace. It hadn't been an uncomfortable silence. It would've been relaxing and more comfortable if his thoughts hadn't been distracted.

There was one thought in particular which kept on niggling him. Once he'd thought of it, it was impossible to push it away. When they'd walked back to the car and were ready to start the drive home, he'd stopped them. He needed to be sure one way or the other.

"Mark, can I borrow your knife" Thomas asked the older man. He could hear the uneasiness in his voice, but he tried to ignore it.

Mark gave him a questioning look as he regarded him for a moment. Then his eyes showed understanding and he nodded at Thomas. "You've got one last doubt you want to prove, don't you son?"

Thomas nodded. "I just need to be sure" he answered. Even as he said it he realized it sounded a little foolish. He'd been brought back from the brink death itself, why shouldn't it be true. Still, he needed to know.

He glanced to the side and saw Ishandra looking at him as he took the knife from Mark. She watched him as he brought the blade to his palm and then hesitated.

"Do you want me to do it?" she asked him.

He shook his head. His nerves tensed at the touch of steel to his skin, but it felt like something he needed to do on his own. He closed his eyes and took a deep breath, then made the move with a quick jerk of his hand. He tensed up as he felt the metal bite into his flesh and he let out a small yelp of pain.

He opened his eyes to see blood running out of the fresh cut. In an odd way he felt a sense of relief at seeing the wound. It wasn't so different, and for a few moments he had a brief sense of hope. The seconds ticked off and once again he saw the flow of blood slow and then stop. He held his breath as the familiar sight of the unnatural healing magic worked upon his body. He saw the flesh knit back together and the wound closed up before his eyes. It'd been so strange to see it happen to Ishandra and then Mark, but seeing it happen to his own body was the hardest of all.

Will A. Sanborn

He stared down at his palm as if it wasn't his own. He just looked at it for several moments as the realization seeped into him, getting him to his very core. There was no denying it now and the understanding numbed him. He felt Ishandra's hand on his arm as he gave the knife back to Mark, but her touch only registered dimly in his consciousness. He watched Mark clean the blade of the knife with a handkerchief. The blood which stained the fabric was all that remained of his injury; it was the only testament to his wound. That's all there would ever be from now on, for how long, eternity? That thought pressed down on him with a cold crushing weight.

They said nothing as they got into the car. They all remained silent, save for Thomas who offered to drive. He wanted something to occupy his mind. Several minutes ticked off, and then Mark broke the silence.

"I know it's a lot to take in Thomas, but you don't have to do it all at once." The older man's voice was low and his message simply stated as he spoke from the back seat.

Thomas glanced up and saw Mark's face looking back at him in the rear-view mirror. Mark's eyes caught his for a brief moment. Thomas didn't say anything, so Mark continued. "I know what you're going through son, I went through it myself all those years ago." He paused, and then added "at least you had some warning..."

"That doesn't help" Thomas replied, his voice sounding hollow. "I don't know what to do now."

"You've got us to help you through it" he heard Ishandra add.

Thomas gave a small nod at that, and then Mark continued. "We're all here for you, and we know you'll be able to get through it. You'll be okay, just like with everything else."

Thomas felt his mood darken again. "But that was nothing compared to this."

"Perhaps everything was to prepare you for this" Thoth interjected. Thomas glanced up to the mirror again to catch the ibis looking at him. "You've shown both courage and the ability to adapt quickly. You've passed every trial put before you."

"I still don't feel all that strong."

"That will come in time, like everything else" Thoth replied. His voice was cool, but not without hints of caring.

"Can I really stay with you guys?" Thomas asked as he glanced at Ishandra.

"Of course, hon. We'd love to have you, and we can help you through this."

"I could stay with you as well" Anubis added, "if you'd want me to..." He heard a touch of uncertainty creeping into the jackal's voice.

He pondered the offer. Again that old vestige of doubt crept up on him. It was one thing to play around with Anubis as a passing diversion on the trip they'd been on, but it was something else completely to ponder a lasting relationship with him. He couldn't think about letting go of the friendships he'd forged with either Ishandra or Anubis though. Even the thought of leaving them left a cold feeling in the pit of his stomach.

"Yes, I think I'd like that, hon" he answered. "I'd like to spend more time with both of you." Even as he said it he couldn't quite believe he did, but it helped to cut through the uncertainty. He caught Anubis' smile in the mirror and it warmed him.

He looked back ahead to the road in front of him. Now that they were finished with the odd quest he wondered what lay ahead. They'd finished the task and he'd done what was required of him, so now they seemed to be headed into an even greater unknown. If he dwelt on it too much the seemingly-infinite expanse of possibilities pushed down upon him with a crushing weight.

He pulled his thoughts back from the wide-open future and tried to focus on the present and the road before him. He had his friends to support him and he was loved. He'd been through so much already that he tried to pretend that being with them was all that mattered. For the moment he managed to do that, and for the moment perhaps that was all that really did matter. He found he was able to smile a little at that thought as they drove along.

Will A. Sanborn

Epilogue: Incognito in Plain Sight

When I finished writing "That Old Time Religion," I had several ideas for stand-alone stories which would be sequels to the novel. There were things I wanted to do with the characters of Ishandra, Thomas and Anubis, and I'd sketched out some scenes to work on. Unfortunately I never go around to writing them up and the energy behind them dissipated.

It wasn't until last year, when I was inspired to write something more to the story. It was November again and I was participating in NaNoWriMo again, but doing a free-form novel as a series of creative writing exercised. I was at the Midwest FurFest convention and watching people at the dance inspired me with this idea. I thought it would be fun to show the immortal characters mixing in with the regular folks at a fantasy convention. The image of Anubis having fun on the dance floor was just too good to pass up, plus it mirrors the scene in the first chapter of the book nicely.

I also wanted to have Thomas and Ishandra talking to show more of where his life had gone. I wanted to show how he had grown from his experiences and how he was adjusting to things. He's more laid back here and is a little different from how I portrayed him in the novel, but he has had time to get used to things, so perhaps he's mellowed out again. Anyways, even though I didn't get all of the scenes I'd originally imagined written down, this little vignette makes a nice epilogue to the story and I think it ends things on a good note.

I had a couple of song lyrics picked out for an epilogue which never got written, but it dealt with some of the similar themes as this story, so I've included them here.

Will A. Sanborn

I looked death in the face last night, I saw him in a mirror
And he simply smiled, he told me not to worry, he told me to take my time
We close our eyes and the world has turned around again
We close out eyes and dream, and another year has come and gone
We close our eyes and the world has turned around again
We close our eyes and dream
  Oingo Boingo, "We Close Our Eyes"

At the end of the tour, when the road disappears
If there's any more people around, when the tour runs aground
And if you're still around, then we'll meet at the end of the tour
The engagements are booked through the end of the world
So we'll meet at the end of the tour
  They Might Be Giants, "The End of the Tour"

The dance was going strong at the convention and the music reverberated through the ballroom with a hard, pulsing beat. The lights flashed in their own rhythm, occasionally finding sync with the baseline, as they illuminated the crowd in random segments. Bodies danced in a wild mesh out on the floor, as the dancers found their own timing to the music.

The black jackal was near the center of the crowd, and he was surrounded by a group of dancers. He was dressed in the garb of an Egyptian god, and they were all too happy to play the act of his loyal followers. He smiled as he danced and moved in close to one person, then another. There were mostly males in his group, but he'd also caught the eyes of a couple of women. He looked like he was favoring the boys, but then he turned and bumped his hips against one of the ladies. She responded in turn when she reached out to take his arm, he accepted her gesture with a happy wag of his tail.

The floor was crowded. There were mostly humans out there, in a wide array of costumes, but a few other exotics could be seen in amongst the sea of bodies as well. There was a female spotted cat of some kind, perhaps an ocelot, as she was petite and lithe. There was also a blue-skinned man in Indian garb, dressed as Krishna. The other people wore costumes in a mix of genres, there were pirates and imperial storm troopers, a lion tamer and his girlfriend in a cat suit. There was also a belly dancer, along with some other animals, using costumes of fake fur and body-paint. Various aliens and generic ravers with glow sticks were sprinkled throughout the crowd. A few people even sported classic masquerade masks with colored feathers. If you looked close, there were probably a couple of ninjas in the mix as well.

At the edge of the dance floor, a few people sat and watched the crowd. A young man and a blue-skinned dragoness were off in the corner. They'd found a spot away from the speakers which wasn't as noisy. They watched the throng of dancing people as they talked. The man was not in costume. He was dressed normally, save for a simple multi-colored shirt, but the dragoness wore the

That Old Time Religion

authentic clothes of a gypsy fortune teller. Her outfit accentuated her body nicely, fitting its form to her shapely curves. She'd received her own share of looks and gestures on the dance floor, but she was being left alone now that she'd moved off to the sidelines with her human friend. Occasionally someone would cast a jealous gaze their way as the two of them were talking.

The man looked out at the jackal dancing in the group. "This was a nice idea, Ishandra" he said. "Anubis is really enjoying himself." He paused a moment, then added "I didn't think I'd have this much fun at a fantasy convention, but it's a nice break."

The dragoness smiled back at him. "It's not too different from the carnival, in a way Thomas. I thought you guys would like it." She winked at him and then also said "so, you've had enough dancing for now?"

He returned her smile. "Yeah, it's okay, but it's not totally my thing and it gets a little tiring. Anubis certainly loves it though... as well as the intention."

She winked at him, "and you're being really good with it too."

"Oh, it's not bad, I know he misses all of his followers back from the old days, and it's kind of fun to watch him eat it all up. It's nice to see him have so much fun too."

She nodded at him and took his hand in hers. "You look like you're having a good time as well."

"Yes, Ishandra, things have been better these past several months, and this weekend has been fun." He paused, and then added. "He's been such a help to me, as were you." He leaned in against her as he said that. "It's also really nice seeing you again."

"Oh Thomas, I'm glad to spend the time with you too. I'd missed you and I'm glad we can all spend the weekend together." She turned to catch his gaze. "I am really glad that the two of you are doing so well together."

"It's surprised me, I have to admit. I wasn't sure about being with him, but we've both been good for each other. A year ago I never would've thought I'd end up with a guy, let alone a god, but then I'd never thought any of that would happen." He blinked his eyes as he felt them start to tear up. He pulled her in close with his arm around her and he felt her own arm hold him tighter.

"I know it's been a lot for you Thomas, but I'm glad you're okay."

She didn't have to say that she was sorry for what he'd been through on their long journey together. They were both beyond that. They had all been affected by what had happened, even if he was the one most changed by it. He had started down the path of acceptance and they could leave those events in the past.

"Yeah, it's been good to get back to school and feel like I have a direction again. I'm talking with my parents more too. They don't know about Anubis of course, that'll have to come later. I'm still not sure about everything, but I guess I have plenty of time to figure that out..."

Ishandra didn't reply to that, but he felt her reassuring presence against him. He continued. "It's still a little odd to be attracted to Anubis and women as well, but he's helping me figure that out. We are having fun together."

He heard her chuckle at that. He gave her side a playful jab with his fingers and was rewarded with her yap of surprise. His jackal wasn't ticklish, so it was nice to have his dragon lover respond in that way, besides, she deserved it.

He let out his own laugh. "I'll get you back for that tonight..."

"Oh, maybe hon" he heard her whisper in his ear, "but remember that you owe me a couple of favors from the last time we were together too..."

He turned his head to face her and they both ended up laughing. When they'd calmed down, they returned their attention back to the dance floor, where Anubis was currently flirting with a guy in a fishnet shirt. Thomas couldn't help but roll his eyes a little at that, but his laugh was warm and genuine.

"I'm glad you're okay with this, and that you're having fun here."

"Yeah, it's cool. I wouldn't have thought I'd be enjoying it as much. It's different, and a bit silly, but everyone is having a good time and it's kind of infectious. Besides, Anubis told me how much he likes to dance, and where else would he fit in so well? He really likes the outfit you found him."

The dragoness grinned at that. "I thought he'd like that. He's really living it up."

"Heh, yeah, he likes being the center of attention. He's letting you spend the night with us, so he can have his fun imagining those glory days again."

"Awww, that's sweet of you. He's certainly a hit here."

"Yeah, he even told me an artist asked him to model for her."

"Oooh, that sounds fun."

Thomas let out a chuckle. "Sure, and we get copies of the pictures too."

He heard her laugh, and then he paused to just watch his exotic lover, who was still dancing up a storm with the friendly crowd. He took in the sight for a few minutes, before he said "Well it's good to see him happy, with everything he's done for me, he deserves to be, and he's fun to spoil like this."

"You deserve to be happy too hon."

He turned back to look at her. "I am, Ishandra. You've both helped me with that." He thought about it for a few moments, and then added "besides, it's fun watching everyone here pretending, while I know I'm the only one who gets to spend time with a couple of real gods."

She met his grin with one of her own. Then she moved in to kiss his smiling lips.

Will A. Sanborn

About the Author

Will Sanborn is a native of New England, and though the winters drag on too long for him, he adores the magic of autumns there. He also loves being within driving distance of both the mountains and the ocean. He works as a digital hardware designer, and builds pieces of "computer chips" for a living. When he's not busy with work or indulging his love of watching movies, he puts his energy into creative projects, including writing and photography.

Will discovered anthropomorphics back in the golden age of the internet. He's been active in the fandom, with writing and conventions, since the early to mid-90s. He found out way back then, that engineers could indeed write fiction, and has enjoyed exploring that playground of the mind ever since. His forte is character-driven stories. He'd much rather write drama or romance, than try and write a bio to describe his own life. Will sometimes plays a raccoon on TV, or at least the internet.

Made in the USA
Lexington, KY
17 July 2011